Ballard Branch

NO LONGER PROPERTY OF
SEATTLE PUBLIC LIBRARY

D0357252

· ANTONIO TABUCCHI ·

For Isabel

A Mandala

Translated by
Elizabeth Harris

archipelago books

First Archipelago Books Edition, 2017

All rights reserved. No part of this book may be reproduced or transmitted
in any form without the prior written permission of the publisher.

Archipelago Books
232 Third Street #A111
Brooklyn, NY 11215
www.archipelagobooks.org

Library of Congress Cataloging-in-Publication Data
Names: Tabucchi, Antonio, 1943-2012, author. | Harris, Elizabeth (Translator), translator.
Title: For Isabel : a mandala
Other titles: Per Isabel. English
Description: First Archipelago Books edition. | Brooklyn, NY : Archipelago Books, 2017.
Identifiers: LCCN 2016051212 | ISBN 9780914671800 (pbk. : alk. paper)
Classification: LCC PQ4880.A24 P4713 2017 | DDC 853/.914--dc23
LC record available at https://lccn.loc.gov/2016051212

Book design and typesetting: Tetragon, London, UK

Distributed by Penguin Random House
www.penguinrandomhouse.com

This book has been published with a translation grant awarded by Italian
Ministry of Foreign Affairs and International Cooperation.

Archipelago Books gratefully acknowledges the generous support from Lannan
Foundation, the National Endowment for the Arts, the New York City Department
of Cultural Affairs, and the New York State Council on the Arts, a state agency.

PRINTED IN THE UNITED STATES OF AMERICA

For Isabel

A Mandala

This book, if considering the mandala, would be dedicated to a woman in the circle of Evocation. But with more earthly considerations, it's dedicated to my friend Tecs, which is not her actual name, though it is what I call her. And along with her, to my old friend Sergio.

Who knows, the dead might have a different custom.

Sophocles, *Antigone*

Justification in the Form of a Note

Private obsessions; personal regrets eroded but not transformed by time, like pebbles smoothed down by the current of the river; incongruous fantasies and the inadequacy of reality. these are the driving principles behind this book. But I also can't deny the influence one summer night of watching a monk dressed in red while he sprinkled colored powder on the bare stone and made me a Mandala of Consciousness. And on that same night, finally getting to a short essay by Hölderlin, which I'd been meaning to read and had carried around in my suitcase for a month. Here's what I underlined in the Hölderlin that night, before the final phase of the moon: "The tragic-moderate weariness of time, whose object is not in fact of interest to the heart, follows the onrushing spirit of time most intemperately, and that spirit then appears wild, not sparing mankind like a spirit by day, but being relentless instead, like the spirit of the eternally living unwritten wilderness and the world of the dead." *

You might find it curious that a writer past fifty, who's published so many books, would still feel the need to justify his adventures in writing. I find it curious myself. Probably, I haven't resolved this issue, if it's a matter of feeling guilty towards the world or simply not working through a loss. Naturally, other explanations are also acceptable. I do want to point out, though, that on that summer night, I happened to fly off to Naples with my imagination, because in that distant sky, there was a full moon. And it was a red moon.

A.T.

---

*   Translated from the German by Shaun Whiteside.

First Circle. Mónica. Lisbon. Evocation.

I 'd never been to Tavares in my entire life. Tavares is the fanciest restaurant in Lisbon, with nineteenth-century mirrors and velvet chairs; the cuisine is international, but they also serve typical Portuguese dishes, though delicately prepared: you might order clams and pork, for instance, what you'd get in Alentejo, and you'll wind up with something more like a Parisian dish, or so I'd been told. But I'd never been, I'd just heard about it. I took a bus to Intendente. The square was full of whores and pimps. It was late afternoon, I was early. I went to an old café I knew, a café with billiard tables, and I started watching a game. An old man with only one leg was leaning on a crutch while he played; his eyes were bright, his hair kinky and grey, and he was hitting pins like there was no tomorrow, he cleaned everybody's clock in the place, then sat down and slapped his belly like he'd just had a good meal.

You want to play, my friend? he asked. No, I answered, I'm sure I'd lose. If you want, though, we could play for a little port, I could use an aperitif, but I'd be glad to offer you one, if you'd prefer. He looked at me and smiled. Your accent's strange, he said, you a foreigner? Somewhat, I answered. Where're you from? he asked. Outside Sirius, I said. I don't know that town, he said, what country's it in? The Great Dog, I said. Huh, he said, so many new countries in the world these days. He scratched his back with his cue. So what's your name? he asked. Waclaw, I answered, but that's just what I was baptized, my friends call me Tadeus. His suspicious look disappeared, and he gave me a wide grin. Then you're baptized, he said, so you're Christian, let me offer *you* a drink, what'll you have? I told him a white port, and he called the waiter over. I know what you need, the man went on, you need a woman, a beautiful African woman, eighteen years old, good price, practically a virgin, just came yesterday from Cape Verde. No thanks, I said, I have to be going soon, I'll be getting a taxi, I have an important appointment tonight, I don't have time for girls right now. He stared at me, puzzled. Hmm, he said, so what're you looking for around here? I lit a cigarette and was quiet a moment. I'm looking for a woman, too, I said, and I'm going around asking about her, I just stopped in here to pass the time, because I have an appointment with a lady who can give me some information, and I want to hear what she has to tell me; actually, I'd better go, there's a taxi free at the stand, I'd better hurry. Wait a second, he said, why're you looking for this woman – do you need her? Maybe, I answered, you might say I lost track of her and I've come from the Great Dog just to look for her, I'd like to know more about her, and that's why I have this appointment. And where is this appointment? he asked. In the most elegant restaurant in Lisbon, I told him, a place full of mirrors and crystal, I've never been, I suppose it'll cost quite a bit, but I'm not the one paying, what can I say, my friend, I'm here on leave, I barely have a coin to my name, so I'd better accept the invitations of others. Is it a fascist place? the old man asked. I couldn't say, I answered, to be honest I never really thought about it in those terms.

I rose quickly, said goodbye, and left. The taxi was still at the stand. I slipped inside and said: good evening, Tavares, please.

We met at the Escravas do Amor Divino boarding school for girls in Lisbon. We were sixteen years old. Isabel was a legend for the entire class because she'd attended the French high school. In that period, you know, the French high school was a place of resistance, all the teachers who taught there couldn't find positions at the public schools because of their anti-fascist beliefs, and going to the French school meant that you knew the world, that you went on field trips to Paris, that you were connected to Europe. We, instead, were from the public high school, a real shithole – pardon the expression – where you studied the Salazarista corporative constitution and the rivers of Portugal and you divided the national poem, *The Lusiads*, into stupid sections, it's a beautiful poem about the sea, but you wound up studying it like some African battle. Because there were colonies back then. But they weren't called colonies; they were called Overseas. Nice name, don't you think? And some people had grown rich from Overseas,

I have to say that was normal for the families of those girls at the boarding school, all seasoned Salazarists, real fascists, but not our parents, I mean mine and Isabel's, another reason, maybe, why we became friends, because our families had this in common. She came from an old Portuguese family that had nothing to do with Salazarism, a family in decline, with property up north, in Amarante, where they make bread in the strangest shapes, but like I said, it was a family with no money or power, their lands up north had all been entrusted to tenant farmers or land agents, with no returns. We spent a few summer vacations, Isabel and I, in their house in Amarante. It wasn't a house, it was a Medieval stone tower, filled with heirlooms and coffers, that overlooked the river, and we were happy there. Those summers were beautiful, back then. Isabel wore a straw hat. Her oval face was even lovelier under this funny hat someone in the family had brought back from Tuscany. And then she'd paint. She was convinced she'd be a painter, and she painted windows. Windows with shutters closed, windows with shutters open, windows with curtains, windows with iron bars, but always windows like those found in Douro or Minho, with their beautiful wooden frames, and often lace curtains. But she never included human beings, they ruin the mystery, she said, see, this window I'm painting is so mysterious with no one there, but if I put in the person who'd be at that window, the mystery would vanish, it's the veterinarian in Amarante, he has a goatee and wears a hairnet while he's sleeping to keep his hair in place, just imagine, he stands by the window and does knee bends, you know, yesterday, while I was painting his window, he showed up and just stood there all stiff at the windowsill, pretending he didn't see me but of course he did see me, he just gazed up toward the heavens, looking inspired, apparently extremely proud to be in my painting, but screw him – I'm not putting him in. And then we'd go for a walk. Just outside Amarante, the river creates channels of still water where frogs breed. We'd spend our mornings fishing for frogs, but in Portugal, people don't know how to fish for frogs because no one eats them, and we came up with a system like boys use for catching lizards. We tied a slip knot in a rush blade, slowly brought the loop over a frog's head, and when it got ready to jump – plop – we caught it. Back then there weren't plastic bags, so we used a mesh bag, the kind for groceries, and the frogs would poke their heads through the mesh, and we were quite the sight, me in my trousers and Isabel in her straw hat from Florence, while we strolled through Amarante carrying our bagful of frogs. People thought we were nuts, which we enjoyed, because at that age you enjoy such things. We'd kill the frogs in the evening, and this became my job, because Isabel refused. Their heads have to be cut off with a quick slice of the knife, and for a few minutes, they kick their legs, headless, as long as their life force continues. Listen, Isabel would say, someday if I kill myself, I think I'll go just like this, with a few kicks, because if you can't cut off your own head, you can always hang yourself, which is something similar, four kicks into empty air, and good-night everybody. We cooked the frogs' legs *à la Provençal*, the way Isabel liked them, because during her time at the French school she'd been to France, to Arles, and she'd eaten frogs' legs *à la Provençal*, with garlic and parsley, and she said it was the best dish in the world. But we soon grew tired of eating frogs' legs *à la Provençal*. Those disturbing little legs, so white and so delicate, almost tasteless, while the rest of the family was eating roast kid and egg soups. And at that age, we had a good appetite. Sure, it's easy to mythologize exotic food eaten in Provence, but then you get hungry. And so we started setting the frogs free in the garden, and the garden grew full of frogs, they were everywhere, in the grass, the bushes, the goldfish pond, the clumps of bamboo. Luckily Isabel's parents had a sense of humor, they didn't mind that invasion, they were always cheerful, open-minded, understanding. Then they died in a car accident, but that's another story, no, it's the same story. Fridays, we went to Barcelos, which had the most beautiful market in the whole region. Maybe you can't picture how beautiful the small-town markets were back then. Or maybe you can. We caught an early-morning bus to Braga, then another from there to Barcelos. The bus arrived around noon. Time enough to wander a little and look at the terracotta ceramics, you know, in Barcelos they make painted terracotta roosters, the symbol of Portugal, and all sorts of other little ceramic things, dolls, typical figurines, nativity sets, musical bands, cats, pitchers, and decorative plates, and then it was time for lunch. We always picked cheap places, taverns filled with regular customers and market vendors. Little old men and little old ladies who came from all over Minho, one looking for a chicken, one wanting to buy a gosling or cow, the quaintest were the brokers, who wore neckerchiefs and drank young wine, they were marvelous, even at their table they acted like they were at the market, screaming, rolling up their sleeves, sweating. It was hot, in Barcelos, and in the tavern, you'd smell the mix of food and the stink of animals off the square, it was beautiful and new for Isabel and me, two girls who spent the year in a city like Lisbon, and we were thrilled; we were fascinated by the brokers, wanted to buy something ourselves, and one day we bought a kid, a sweet little creature, black and white, with spots on his muzzle and delicate legs; we rode home on the bus with him in a large basket, and because he wasn't weaned, for a time we fed him milk from a bottle. We put him in the garden, made him a leaf hut, and in the mornings, when we went shopping in Amarante, we led him around on a leash. I can't begin to describe the looks we got, me in my trousers and Isabel in her straw hat from Florence, no bag of frogs now, just a little goat on a leash, and what's more, at the bakery, Isabel wanted to buy that bread in the shape of a male organ, like they make in Amarante, only it's the servants who buy that bread for making canapés, and we bought it just to get attention, and we stuffed our bag full of these loaves, it was scandalous, everyone staring at us, even that fitness fanatic of a veterinarian wouldn't show up at the window anymore. In other words, it was a hoot. And then the summers ended. They ended because we wound up at the university No, really, because Isabel's parents had died. Like I said, they died in a car accident. On Póvoa de Varzim Road, after lunch, after Isabel's papa had a lot to eat and drink. No one knows who was to blame, because it was a head-on collision. But I think Isabel's papa had drunk too much, because I knew him, he liked to drink. They didn't die right away. They were in a coma for three days then died at the same time, he and his wife. Funny, don't you think? Both of them going into a coma and then dying at the same time because there was nothing else to do: the heart stops beating and that's when the doctors pull out the tubes. But that's what happened. Isabel and I spent three days and three nights at the hospital in Oporto, in the intensive care unit. The nurse let us sleep in a side-room, and now and then we'd slip into their rooms. Papa, Papa, it's me, Isabel would say, Mama, do you hear me? – do you remember the frogs we brought back to the house in Amarante, me and my friend, Mónica, look, we want to get more next summer, come on, Mama, wake up, come out of this goddamned coma, I want you to smile at me, to tell me what to wear, like before, to scold me *parce que je ne suis pas parfaite* the way you'd like, I need you to, Mama. But her mama didn't scold her anymore and neither did her father. They died together, like I told you, in the exact same hour, and we arranged the funeral. Isabel had them buried in the same shrine, in a village cemetery out in the countryside surrounding Amarante. When we went to the funeral, it was a beautiful, warm, sunny October day. Isabel was dressed in dark blue and I wore a beige dress that made me look older than her. You see? Isabel said when we got back from the cemetery, they went away, and you know what, Mónica, it's over now, no more summers with frogs, no more eating out in Barcelos, childhood's over, they're gone now, I'm an orphan, and I think you're something of an orphan yourself. And I did feel like I was something of an orphan myself. Because Isabel's parents were real parents, what mine never were. My father was always off on trips in his Mercedes-Benz, away on business, like we'd say at home, and my mother had her own friends and engagements. And so I was left feeling like something of an orphan myself. The walks to the river, the old house in Amarante, the dream summers: all over. We met again at the university, but it wasn't the same. I was majoring in classics, a choice which, in the ideological division that existed then at the University of Lisbon, was considered conservative. And it's true: the classics students didn't do anything, they never called any meetings, they never even went to the cafeteria, where most real discussions took place. Isabel majored in modern languages, and that major, yes, that one had some life to it. One professor taught a course on Camus and existentialism, another, a course on surrealism in Portugal, and there were even poets from that illustrious movement who came and read their work, I can't remember who anymore, but they were well-known, and it was a real triumph, the assembly hall was packed, I remember Isabel, who'd become a leader and introduced the poets to the students, there were even kids sitting on the floor, not that those poets spoke out directly against fascism, this just wasn't possible, but their poems were nonconformist, in some ways, revolutionary, revolutionary in quotes, though, because back then, everything was in quotes. Isabel stepped onto the stage in her pink scarf, and this too was a sign: back then, you couldn't use red, you had to use a color tied to red, and that was a sign. It felt strange seeing

Isabel again, up on the stage in that assembly hall; she spoke with ease, maybe a slight nervous inflexion to her voice, she read her biographical notes on the poets, and she said: two free-verse poets who honor us, because today free-verse is banished. And a thunderous applause broke out, one of the poets rose to his feet and read a surrealist poem mocking bourgeois values, and the audience went crazy, then the other poet went up and read an homage to Garcia Lorca, murdered by the fascists – you might laugh today, but back then, something like this was a great political event, you probably know this better than me, Portugal was a country forgotten by Europe and forgetful of Europe, we were closed off on a dead-end street, in a sort of moldering monastery whose sexton was António de Oliveira Salazar. And everything unfolded as in a monastery: conventions, habits, rituals, when kids got together in someone's home, subdued, melancholy gatherings. Sometimes Isabel would organize *fado castiço* sessions in her home, I mean the aristocratic fado, as you know, and this too was one of Isabel's contradictions, meetings with revolutionaries at the university and aristocratic fados at home, but I liked those sessions, I went to some, I remember Thereza de Noronha showed up one time – for us she was a legend – she came from an old aristocratic family and sang old fados in a proud voice, Isabel would light the candles on the table in the living room, there was port for everyone, and we listened solemnly to the singer, the aristocratic fadista, a shawl covering her shoulders, all of us there, in veneration, around the candles and the port. We were celebrating a rite and we all knew it, and meanwhile the world kept rushing along, the world outside, but in those gatherings of hers, we didn't seem to notice. Isabel wore mauve-colored sweaters crocheted by her nanny, who'd remained with her, an elderly lady who was once her wet nurse, she took the place of Isabel's parents, she came from Beira Baixa and still had a strong provincial accent in spite of all her years in Lisbon, she's the one who knows everything about Isabel, she was close to Isabel during her most difficult years, such devotion, but I think I might be rambling, am I rambling? Well, it doesn't matter, anyway, you can go ask her nanny, I'm not the one who knows the most about Isabel, at this point, I only know what I've heard. About that love affair. But I repeat: I practically lost track of Isabel. I have a feeling that affair was the ruin of her, that's where it all began, I mean, where her end began. But I'm only telling you what

I heard. It seems she met a foreign boy at school, I couldn't say what nationality, Andalusian, I think. The one thing I am sure of: he had a scholarship. Sometimes I'd see them together, because they were always together, now that I think about it, he was definitely Spanish, I don't remember anymore, so many years have passed. The three of us had dinner once at Toni dos Bifes, a small restaurant near Campo Pequeno which cost next to nothing, the cooking was simple, but the portions were large, and Isabel and her boyfriend were regulars. I remember that evening well. Isabel was very excited because there was an important writer at a nearby table with the entire editorial staff of the journal *Almanaque*. They'd often meet up at Toni dos Bifes. Back then, this journal was legendary for making fun of everything and everyone: the country and its institutions, the bourgeoisie, Portugal's traditions and maritime discoveries, which it bragged about so much; this was something of an underground journal, popular with young people and nonconformists, and Isabel was young and wanted to be a nonconformist. Then the writer saw the foreign boy and said hello, no, actually, he got up and came over to our table. He held out his hand in greeting. He was short and stocky and resembled a peasant; to look at him, you'd never say he was a sophisticated writer, but that's how writers are – deceptive. We were eating steak and eggs, the cheapest thing on the menu, and the writer asked us if we wanted to join him at his table. So we carried our plates over, and the *Almanaque* editorial staff offered us a tray of duck rice, telling us that young people needed their nourishment. Then the writer and the foreign boy started talking about Vittorini and Italian Neorealism, Isabel chimed in now and then, she'd read *Men and Not Men* and admired the Italian Resistance, yes, I remember clearly, Isabel's boyfriend was definitely Spanish, he had all the features of an Andalusian, the jet-black hair, the sharp nose of the gypsy or Sephardic Jew. He called Portuguese girls "annoying pests," and the writer jumped on the opportunity to change the topic to Sá-Carneiro, who called the bourgeois parasites, no, better, lepidopterans. And so the evening ended with a conversation about lepidopteranism, and each staff editor thought up a different category of lepidopterans. Listening to soccer on the radio was lepidopteran, going to the beach on Sundays was lepidopteran, eating baccalà was lepidopteran, going to confession was lepidopteran, dressing in black was lepidopteran, getting up early was lepidopteran, eating in expensive restaurants was lepidopteran, keeping a diary was lepidopteran. And so on. It was the evening of lepidopteranism. When we left, Isabel asked me, of the two of us, who was more lepidopteran. I said I was. And it was true. I was more bourgeois, the one tied to customs and tradition. Isabel had gone her own way by then, had practically become a stranger, I didn't recognize her anymore, she'd practically become a stranger, even to me, maybe we no longer had anything to say to one another. And in fact she wasn't the one who told me about that affair of hers, like I told you, that was the rumor going around at school. As far as I'm concerned, it's all a lie; there have always been those who gossip, but in those terrible years the gossip was especially cruel. Apparently, the Spanish student was friends with a Polish writer, whom he introduced to Isabel. A friendship sprang up. A friendship between the three of them, but in my opinion, that's all it ever was, a friendship, picnics on the beaches of Ericeira, Sunday ferry rides on the Tagus, trying to avoid being lepidopterans, and things along that line. In my opinion, the reason Isabel did it was exactly that, to avoid being a lepidopteran, to show everyone the free, uninhibited woman she desired to be, and maybe wasn't – but who knows. So anyway I heard it said around school that apparently there were complications. I say apparently because I can't be sure, but a student whispered it to me, a girl who barely knew her, a communist girl Isabel spent time with, probably to keep from feeling lepidopteran, a little fanatic and a moralist besides, like the communists were back then, and she told me: apparently, Isabel's pregnant, but no one knows if the father's the Spaniard or the Pole. And then she made it clear that Isabel had joined the Communist Party, and this was why she wasn't around anymore, she was living a semi-underground existence, because she was writing for *Avante* under the pseudonym Magda, I think, or something like that. But what could Isabel write for the communist paper? I asked, what could she possibly write with the childhood she had, with her background, with the life she's led? She writes appeals to the democratic youth, that idiot girl answered, she's become our biggest ideologue, her articles are like cracks of the whip, invocations, rallies, she's great, your friend, but now she's in trouble. And I didn't see Isabel from then on. Once in a while, I heard about her from that idiot communist girl who wound up leaving for Angola to fight on the side of the liberation front, and was never seen again, good for her, I can't even remember her name, Fátima, maybe, and she told me: you know, Isabel decided to have an abortion, everyone abandoned her, except her nanny and us, her comrades, but her nanny didn't know anything about this ugly business. And I said: honey, you're kind of an idiot, I know Isabel better than you do, these stories you're telling me seem to come right out of this underground life you lead, look, that's not Isabel's nature, being underground, everything she's ever done has been in the light of day, so you can go screw yourself, you and your party. I never saw Isabel again. But I did see that idiot communist girl again, sometime later, and she told me: Isabel's depressed, it looks like her troubles made her fall into a depression, I'm not able to contact her, they say she went to live in a small town up north, do you know how to track her down? I tried calling her in Amarante, but her nanny answered, Isabel wasn't there, she didn't know where to find her, and then she said: Mónica, dear Mónica, if you do manage to learn something about Isabel, won't you please tell me, I'm terribly worried, I wanted to contact the police but some friends of hers called, people I didn't know, and they told me not to contact the police, even if she doesn't show up, it might be a matter of life or death, I'm in such a state, I want to hear my Isabel's voice, I don't know where she is or what she's doing, and it's killing me. And making that phone call killed me a little, too. What had happened to Isabel? Where did she wind up? Why had she disappeared? And then: was the idiot communist girl's story true? And if it was true, Isabel would need someone to help her, and keep her company, and comfort her. And I was the only one who could do this, I was her old friend, her true friend who'd known her since she was a girl, how could she have forgotten everything, our friendship, our summers in Amarante, the frogs? And so I began to try and track her down. I got in touch with a friend of the idiot communist girl, who meanwhile had left for Africa. This guy was young but going bald, a student who'd taken too long to finish and never went to classes anymore but still diligently frequented the cafeteria. He participated in a lot of underground activities; it was so obvious, I was amazed the secret police hadn't identified him yet. But the secret police, who seemed to be very informed, were also pretty stupid, they couldn't manage to oversee the university, so the balding kid eluded them. I stopped him one day in the cafeteria. I got behind him in line and said at his back: I'm a friend of Isabel's, I want to know what's happened to her. We were at the self-service counter, choosing our food, and he didn't react, you could see he was accustomed to this sort of secrecy, he turned to the serving woman behind the counter and said: the baccalà doesn't look fresh, I'll take the hake with herbs, and then he went on as if he were still ordering: Isabel has some mental problems, she's hiding out, I can't give you her contact information, sorry. Go screw yourself, I said, and grabbed my plate. And that was the last I heard anyone speak of Isabel. And then a week later I saw the notice in the *Diário de Notícias*, the only morning paper, as you know, so there's not exactly a lot of choices It read: the friends of Isabel Queriz do Monte announce that it is God's will to call into his Divine presence his beloved daughter Isabel, for whom the Seventh Day Mass will be celebrated at eleven o'clock, tomorrow morning, the eighteenth of April, in the church of Encarnação, in Cascais. The following day, I went to Cascais. It was a glorious day. I walked around the entire bay and stopped at a coffee shop. I'd arrived early and had to wait a short while, the bay was filled with sailboats ready for the regatta, I walked all along the bay, smoked a cigarette, thought about Isabel, prepared myself spiritually, and I went to the Encarnação, a small church with the most beautiful panoramic view of Cascais. In front of the church, a fishmonger was selling shellfish off a small cart. I bought some and started eating them raw while I sat and waited on a stone bench. At a quarter to eleven, I realized no one else was coming. I waited a little longer and ate my shellfish, and then I went into the church. The Encarnação is less a church than a sailors' chapel. There are old ex-votos and the pulpit is dominated by a Madonna some sailor painted long ago, during his travels. I settled onto a kneeling stool and waited. At eleven o'clock, the parish priest arrived along with two altar boys, and before celebrating the Mass, the priest spoke only to me: this is the Seventh Day Mass for our dear sister Isabel whom Our Lord has called. After the Mass, I found him in the vestry. Father, I said, I'm an old friend of Isabel's, I'd like to know how she died. He looked at me, his eyes wide with astonishment, and said: I don't know, myself – I was only assigned the task of celebrating the Seventh Day Mass, but I don't know how she died. And you don't know where she's buried? I asked, or who these friends of hers are?

I don't know, he said, I truly don't. But you did know Isabel, didn't you? I asked. Of course, he answered, I met her as a child, and these last few years, she came to me for confession. And what did she have to say? I asked. I can't possibly tell you, my dear, he answered, because of the secrecy of the confession. But do you know how she died and where her body lies? I asked. He removed his stole and looked at me, his expression desolate. I don't know, he answered, I don't know anything, they told me she was dead, and I believed them, some of her university friends called me and gave me an offering for the Seventh Day Mass, but I didn't see Isabel after she died, and I don't know where she's buried, I don't know why you're asking me, since her friends know – aren't you her friend? I am, I told him, but lately she had more contact with these friends who led such obscure lives – you know how it is in this country, Father – I haven't managed to learn a thing. I went out to the Cascais bay. It was past noon, a sparkling April. I stopped at a restaurant and ordered grilled fish. The waiter brought me my fish and asked if I wanted to take a tour up to the Mouth of Hell. I told him I didn't like tours. That's all I found out about Isabel. There were rumors going around that she'd committed suicide, but those rumors weren't credible, they were spread by people at the university who knew as much as me. The balding boy disappeared, and like I said, the idiot communist girl left for Angola. The only person who might be able to tell you something more, if she's still alive, is her nanny, Beatriz Teixeira, she goes by Bi, she should still be at her old address, in Travessa da Palmeira, I don't know the exact number, but anyone on the street could point it out. I repeat: if she's still alive. There's nothing more I can tell you.

Second Circle. Bi. Lisbon. Orientation.

S ince I never saw you at the house in Amarante, and you
claim you knew Isabel, that means you met her later,
when she was already a woman, even if for me she was
never a woman, she was always my little girl. My name is Beatriz,
Beatriz Teixeira, but she called me Bi, and I was always her Bi,
like she called me when she was little and kept calling me: Bi. I
can still hear her little girl voice, when she was ill: Bi, Bi, I want
you, I want you to keep me company, I want my Bi. And then I'd
climb the stairs and bring her a toy, a glass of orange juice, a little
homemade treat. From the time she was little she was always ill,
she suffered from asthma. It was a predicament, because asthma's
not curable, it's more a symptom than a disease, and there was

really nothing to be done. Her mother was desperate. Then I took it upon myself to consult a homeopathic doctor, my cousin's son, a good boy who worked at Santa Maria Hospital and practiced regular medicine, but in the afternoons he cured patients by his own methods. He came and saw her and said: it's psychosomatic asthma, this child has psychological problems, I couldn't tell you what sort, you'd need a psychologist, but she definitely has mental problems. I could diagnose her: for someone like me who knew her, it didn't take much. Her father wasn't around, was never around during that time; he was always in Paris, and when he was home, it was more like he wasn't. Isabel would pester me: Bi, did Papa write?, Bi, did Papa call?, Bi, when's Papa coming home? She missed her father, she was a little in love with him, like all girls are at that age. Poor man, you had to understand: there was more debt than revenue from the property in Amarante, a friend of his in Paris had proposed that he get involved with a French import-export company that had dealings with Portugal, he'd sold off some hectares of land and was working hard to get by. You could really feel his absence. And Isabel's mother wasn't exactly a great help to the child. She was too involved with her parish.

During those times, there happened to be a priest in one of the most elegant parish churches of Lisbon who'd got it into his head to go against the rules of the patriarch, the Cardinal, who was an important fascist, God help us. In those times, going against these rules was madness, because the Cardinal and Salazar were one and the same, they'd grown up together, Salazar was even the Cardinal's sexton, and this parish priest – a good man, certainly, but also rather full of himself – started tilting at windmills. And so one day, the secret police arrived in the parish and told him: if you'd please come with us. In some circles in Lisbon, people grew anxious, because any harm to that priest meant harm to certain Catholics who counted a great deal in public opinion. How is it, these Catholics wondered, how is it that a parish priest like this can wind up in prison because from his pulpit, he preached against the Pharisees? It's in the Gospel. And they started to form committees in his defense. And heading one of these committees was Isabel's mother. Perhaps she had a weakness for that priest, he was a handsome man, I have to admit: tall, olive-skinned, jet-black, pomaded hair, he'd sometimes come to our home for tea and Isabel's mother would shower him with attention. When he was arrested, madam treated the news as a catastrophe. Dear madam, I told her, what's one more arrest, Peniche Fort is filled with political prisoners, half the country's in prison, dear madam, maybe a priest is just what's needed, he can hear confessions and comfort the prisoners. But she wouldn't listen to reason. All day long on the telephone with friends, with the committee, with the patriarchate secretary, and then in the evenings, endless gatherings at a women's club along Avenida Duque de Loulé, where all the elegant ladies in Lisbon went. Isabel stayed home alone with me every night, she was afraid to go to bed, and I'd put her to bed. But she didn't want fairy tales or stories to fall asleep to, besides, she wasn't a baby anymore, she was a girl now, a very beautiful girl. She told me the strangest things. She told me: grownups always find a lover, who knows, maybe Papa found a lover in Paris, but my mama, she found an ideal lover, but she'd never have the courage to make love with him, because he's a priest who only thinks about the Pharisees, in my opinion, that priest's a total idiot. And I'd tell her: Isabel, a girl like you mustn't say such things. And she'd answer: Bi, you've always lived with us and I'm sure you've never been with a man, you've never had a lover, but when the time comes, I'm going to find myself a lover, I'll pick a man who's full of himself, like the men Mama knows, I'll make him fall head over heels in love with me and I'll make him die from unhappiness. And I'd tell her: you mustn't talk about such things, you're just a girl, these things are for grownups, you're my little one, don't think such things, Isabel. And she insisted: that's not true, I'm almost grown, I'll find a lover and I'll make him die from unhappiness. And there you have it: that was my Isabel.

She'd spoken in one long breath. She grew quiet and looked at me. Only then did I realize that she must be ancient. She was a decrepit storehouse of memories.

Dear Madam Teixeira, I said, your story is filled with affection, and I know you felt great affection for Isabel, but this isn't enough for me, I'd like to learn other things. She looked at me suspiciously. I don't know what else I could tell you, she answered, I was only her nanny. Well, I said, it couldn't have escaped her nanny that Isabel had problems with the police – serious problems – and that it was the secret police. She looked at me even more suspiciously. Who told you that? she asked. Mónica told me, I answered. Of course, she said, Miss Mónica, and then: but why didn't you ask Miss Mónica? Because Mónica knows less than you, dear Bi, I said, if you'll permit me to call you this, and she insists you were taking care of Isabel when the secret police were looking for her. Miss Mónica told you this? Bi asked. Mónica told me this, I confirmed, why deny it?, please don't deny it, dear Bi, otherwise you'll just have to take it back. I take back nothing, Bi said, as if she'd been greatly accused, I certainly don't take back that time when Isabel needed me. So tell me about that time, I said. She poured herself a glass of water from the pitcher on the table. One night, she whispered, Isabel started knocking on my door, it must have been midnight, and she said, Bi, the police are looking for me, it was raining, she was soaked. The old woman paused. And so? I said. Please don't interrupt me, she said. I let her talk.

It was raining, her hair was wet, she was soaked. Bel, I said, my Bel, what do you mean, the police? But she wouldn't say anything more. And me, following her, asking: but what do you mean, the police?, why the police?, what's happened? And her, quiet. And me, getting her a bowl of hot soup, insisting: what've you been up to that the police are looking for you?, what sort of affair is this – is it something political? Silly Bi, she answered, of course it's something political, now, no more questions, and if someone's looking for me, I'm not here, you don't know where I am, maybe someone will come and tell you he's a contact, he's a friend, I'll be gone all day, now and then I'll come here and sleep. But one afternoon, some men arrived. The secret police. They looked all over, arrogant men, asking me all kinds of questions. You know where she is, tell us, they demanded. I told them I knew her when I was employed in her home, and I didn't know anything about her anymore. So who sleeps here? they said, looking around the small room where Isabel slept. My friend, I lied, Maria da Conceição, she was a pastry chef who used to work for rich people in their homes, but now she's retired. And then that night, when Isabel returned, I told her everything. She collected her small bag, which she'd hidden and, luckily, the police hadn't found, inside were leaflets and books, if my contact comes looking for me, she said, tell him I've gone to stay with a friend, a girl I trust, and she kissed me and left, and I haven't seen her since.

She breathed deeply and poured herself another glass of water. I haven't seen her since, she repeated. That might be the case, I answered, but you must have seen her death notice in the paper, I can't imagine no one told you. Old Bi glanced at me sideways over her glasses. What death notice? she asked. For the Seventh Day Mass at the Cascais Chapel, I answered. Did Miss Mónica tell you this as well? she asked. Mónica went to the chapel that day, I said, but no one was there. Someone's idea of a joke, she answered, you always find morons putting that sort of thing in the paper. So, I said, Isabel didn't commit suicide. The very idea, she said, you think my little Bel's someone who'd kill herself – with her strength of character? And so? I asked. And so? she said. And so where did she end up? She stretched her arms wide. Where destiny took her, she said. But do you know how to find her? I asked, do you know where she is? The very idea, she sighed. And then she added: excuse me, sir, but even if I did know, do you really think I'd tell you when I've never laid eyes on you before? – and why are you so interested, anyway? It's a private matter, I answered, and would take too long to explain.

We seemed to be at a stalemate. If Bi didn't know, it was useless for me to keep on insisting. If she did know, it was equally useless for me to keep on insisting, she'd never give out any news of her Bel to some stranger who'd shown up at her door years later. And then I said: Mónica only knows so much, in that period, she barely saw Isabel anymore, but you, dear Bi, you must know who Isabel spent time with while she was in hiding at your home. Her contact, she said at once, she saw her contact. And who was her contact? I asked, what did he look like? No idea, she said. All right, I said, you have no idea, but still, there must be someone you did know that Isabel saw back then. She seemed lost in thought. There was a female musician, she said, back then, Isabel spent time with a female musician who lived on Travessa do Carmo, but I don't know where she lives now, she plays modern music, and has a foreign name, I've heard she plays at a club on Praça da Alegria, you know, that music Negros invented, I don't know what it's called, and I don't remember that girl's name anymore, either, a foreign name. And now, goodnight to you, excuse me, these days I go to bed early.

Third Circle. Tecs. Lisbon. Absorption.

L isbon Sundays, like some Lisbon Sundays can be, when a thick, Atlantic fog rolls in and chokes the city. Mornings, what do you do?, you go to Mass at São Domingos, my friend told me, and afternoons, you get caught in a little rain and wind up twiddling your thumbs.

That's what happened to me. But I didn't go to Mass, I got caught in a little rain and wound up twiddling my thumbs. Finally, evening came.

I left by way of Alexandre Herculano and walked along Avenida da Liberdade. I stopped in front of the window of an airline company, where there was an enormous poster on display, an invitation to visit the desert. At that hour, Lisbon, too, was practically a desert. I hadn't eaten, and I wasn't hungry, all I needed to do was get up my nerve. I stopped in front of the Hotel Tivoli and thought of going into the bar, maybe it would do me some good, I used to know an old bartender there named Joaquim.

He was behind the bar, in his bowtie, but he didn't seem to recognize me. Good evening, Joaquim, I said, don't you recognize an old friend? He studied me, his face neutral. A friend is always a friend, he answered philosophically. He was serving an elegant American couple. I settled onto a stool, then changed my mind and sat down at a small table in the corner. Joaquim came right over. What may I bring you? he asked with great politeness. He clearly didn't recognize me. Listen, Joaquim, I told him, you might not know me now, but you used to, never mind, my friend, that's how life goes, for a bartender, though, you don't have much of a memory, usually bartenders have an excellent memory, the memory of an elephant.

Joaquim had inconceivable resources. A bartender must never recognize his customers, he said, since he never knows if they'll appreciate it or not, and he set a small bowl of peanuts down on my table, do you want the usual? I looked at him, curious, and he remained unflappable. Just to check his memory, I answered: okay, the usual. And I stretched my legs beneath the table. Joaquim came back and asked me to excuse him. Pardon my bad service, he said, face impassive, but that American couple is dreadful, they only drink American whiskey, as if that's all that exists in the whole wide world, I finished the bottle and had to find another in the storeroom.

Carefully, he set a not quite full martini glass on the table, and topped it off from a small crystal pitcher. Vodka and lemon, he murmured, because, if I'm not mistaken, orange juice gives you acid stomach, plus, a drop of angostura bitters. He carefully stirred the glass with a small spoon and added: did I remember correctly? Joaquim, you're absolutely splendid, I said, how is it you remember so well? – so much time has passed. The memory of an elephant, he replied, a requirement for any bartender. And then he continued: and your friend Ruy, what became of him?, he liked the same drink. His spirit must be in Timor, I answered, that's what he deserves since he spent his best years there, but his body lies here in the city, in the British Cemetery. I'm sorry, Joaquim said, he wrote beautiful poetry, I'm truly sorry. He asked if he could sit down. Of course, Joaquim, I said, by all means, sit, and we'll have a chat. It looks like those two are getting plastered, he whispered, pointing to the American couple, and then he asked: so your friend, Ruy, was he Portuguese or Timorese? He wrote in Portuguese, I said, but his narrow eyes and his love for lullabies, he got from Timor. I remember he came in here once and cried, Joaquim said, he was crying because Portugal lost Timor. Before he died, I said, he sent me one of his poems that I translated into Polish, want me to read it to you? Unfortunately, I don't understand Polish, Joaquim replied, it's a language I never learned. I meant I'd read it in our language, I said, it's here in my pocket. I pulled out my wallet and removed a piece of paper, folded over twice. You know what, Joaquim, I said, it's called "Poetic Condition," and I think it's about all of us, but me in particular, because where I come from, I find myself in a similar condition. I cleared my throat and read: I am so tired of you, they praise you, oh, poetry!, we go everywhere together, wake up together in the same bed, we've composed songs, created children; now chased by dogs and dew drops, we return to the promised land, sacred mountains, mysterious dawn, calm sunrise in granite, wake up, spirit, and celebrate the sun fast that embraces us and melts away.

I looked at Joaquim, and he looked at me. It's quite beautiful, he said, it gave me the shivers, you know, it made me think back to one of those summer days from my childhood, where all you saw were cork oaks, and the sun was relentless. The sun fast that embraces us and melts away – not bad, huh, Joaquim? I said. Not bad, he agreed, I'd like to understand poetry, but I chose this line of work, I serve spirits. In my view, poetry's not much different from spirits, I said, trying to be of some comfort. You think so? he said, you want a little more vodka? No, I said, maybe a little absinthe, like they used to drink in the nineteenth century, there was a bar I once knew, in Bairro Alto, where you could get absinthe, who knows if it's still around, though. You can still find absinthe, Joaquim said, I know this little factory in Minho that makes it, only a few bottles, but there are bars around here that have it, I don't think it's banned in Portugal, you know, we're not at all like the rest of Europe. What do you mean, Joaquim? I asked. That we hold onto our independence, he said with pride. Sure, I answered, when it comes to absinthe, anyway. And what fine plans do you have for this evening? Joaquim went on. I'm going to a club nearby, I said, in Praça da Alegria, I'm going to listen to some jazz. Who knows, Joaquim said, maybe you'll find some absinthe, I've heard they serve it around there. How much do I owe you, my friend? I asked. He held up his hands. I insist, he said, if you'd allow me, after so many years. I also insist, I replied. Listen, he said, consider it a gift, from the Tivoli, if you wish, the Tivoli's still a high-class hotel, but above all, consider it a gift from my elephant memory. And he shook my hand.

The *Hot Dog* was a tiny place, with one long bar and a few tables. Luckily, it wasn't very crowded. I wasn't in the mood that night for a crowd. But perhaps on that foggy Sunday evening, Lisboners weren't much interested in listening to jazz. A poster on the door read: Tecs on saxophone. And then, below: A Tribute to Sonny Rollins.

I sat down at a corner table. The waiter hurried over and asked if I wanted to eat right away or wait until after the performance. It depends how long it goes, I answered. It's just two pieces, he said, tonight the saxophonist will only be playing two pieces, she's tired, yesterday was Saturday and she played until three in the morning. I decided to eat after the performance, and the waiter asked me if I wanted an aperitif. I'd like an absinthe, I said. He didn't bat an eye as he replied: on the rocks or straight? Why? I asked, is absinthe also served on the rocks? It is here, he said, in our bar, it's served on the rocks. Straight, I said, just to be contrary, I want a serious absinthe, like they used to drink in the old days.

The piano and the double bass were already tuning up. The waiter disappeared and the lights dimmed. The saxophonist came in through a small side door and leaned against the bar. She had grey hair, but you could tell she was still young. I liked her right away: she had a determined expression, a face slightly marked by time, and blue eyes. Her saxophone was hanging by a leather strap around her neck. She settled her elbows behind her on the bar, looked around, and said: tonight, I'm playing a tribute to Sonny Rollins, just two tunes, the first is called, "Everything Happens to Me."

She began to play, softly, and then with more power. I knew it was a traditional song, a ballad transformed into jazz. It was romantic and intimist, with some short improvisations that Tecs handled well. I paid close attention; though the music didn't speak to me, I paid close attention. When she finished, there was brief clapping from the connoisseurs, and I clapped, too. The lights went up and the waiter arrived with my absinthe. A break, he said, a ten-minute break, the musician's tired tonight. I thanked him, then stopped him from leaving with my hand. Listen, I said, would you mind letting the saxophonist know that after the second piece, I'd like to chat with her, and that I'd be delighted if she'd consider having dinner with me, please tell her I'm an old friend of Isabel's.

The waiter left and the lights dimmed again. Tecs showed up and went back to her spot by the bar. Before she started, she said: "Three Little Words." And then she began to play. It seemed like a movement in four parts, I was no expert, but this was what they called hard-bob, hard, like they played in the Sixties, and she was adding some swing, with something just a touch romantic. The audience clapped and I clapped, too. The lights went up. I laid my napkin on my lap and waited. A short while later, Tecs arrived. She'd changed into a blue top. You wanted to see me? she said. I'm an old friend of Isabel's, I told her, would you care to join me for dinner? She sat down at my table. What are you drinking? she asked. She had a strong English accent. I'm drinking absinthe, I answered, but straight, I had some vodka earlier, it's probably a deadly combination. And what will you be eating? she asked. Fried eggs and pancetta, I said. How's that sound? Like a deadly combination, she answered, but you go right ahead, I'll have a shrimp salad.

The waiter came over, a pleasant smile on his face. We ordered our eggs and salad. Saxophone music started playing softly over the intercom. Is that you, too? I asked. She said it was. It's my tribute to Sonny Rollins, she said. A disk I cut last month. Were you already playing when you met Isabel? I asked. You're making me go back in time, Tecs sighed. I was strictly a beginner then, I was attending the university, and once in a while I'd play at the student canteen. A strange story, I said, a British girl studying in Lisbon and playing saxophone at the university. American, she corrected me, I'm American, and my story's no stranger than anyone else's: my father was an engineer in Norfolk, and his firm offered him work in the Lisbon shipyards, my mother wanted to get to know Europe, my father accepted the job, and we came to Portugal, I enrolled in the College of Sciences, I'm a biologist, actually, though I've never worked in this field, and I was already studying the saxophone then, though I was timid, Isabel's the one who discovered that I played and insisted I perform at the university canteen; for those Portuguese kids, listening to jazz was revolutionary, the music of a great democratic country, here in Portugal the regime supported Fado, and one singer in particular who had a beautiful voice, I won't deny it, the regime turned her into propaganda, and she turned the regime into propaganda herself, it was awful. I think I know the singer, I said. Of course you do, she said, we all do, there's no point in naming names. And Isabel? I asked. Isabel was in a student organization, Tecs said, students against the regime, she suggested I join too, and I did, but I was shielded by my American passport, it wasn't as dangerous for me as it was for her, the truth is, that organization didn't do anything, people just read banned political books, not much else, but Isabel hung out with other people she didn't introduce me to, then she disappeared for a while, then later I learned she'd been arrested and was in Caxias Prison, we heard news of her from a prison guard who risked coming to the university and giving us a note, he was a prison guard in the opposition, who aided political prisoners. Tecs grew quiet and then went on: so much time has passed. And then she said: and meanwhile, I went off to America for a bit, and when I returned, they told me Isabel had died, that she committed suicide in prison, and they showed me her death notice in the paper, and that's everything I know.

We both were quiet. The record had ended, too. The only sound was the soft murmuring of the last customers at their tables. You know, Tecs, I said, there's no death certificate for Isabel, I looked for it in the municipal archives. What do you mean? she asked. Just this, I answered, that officially, she never died. But they told me she killed herself in prison, Tecs said, that she swallowed glass. I understand, I answered, but all sorts of things can be said. But I saw her death notice in the paper, she insisted, I saw it with my own two eyes. And you always believe what you see in the papers? I asked, and besides, anyone could put in a death notice. That's true, she admitted, but what are you planning to do? I'd like to find that prison guard you mentioned, I said, maybe he knows something, do you remember his name? Tecs put her face in her hands. Oh God, she said, I used to know it, but that was a long time ago. Go on and try, I encouraged her, we have all night. Tecs looked at me and shook her head. Sorry, she told me, I've blocked it out, all I remember is that he was from Cape Verde. That's not much, I said, try a little harder. I don't remember anything else, she answered, I'm sorry. Listen, Tecs, I said, that man's important to me, so you have to try, and, might I add that absinthe doesn't just make a person feel elated, it also brings on a remarkable clear-headedness – what would you say to a glass? She smiled. I've never tried it, she said, I don't know how it might affect me. And then she went on: but who cares, the night's pretty much over, I'll have one. I called to the waiter, and something else occurred to me. Sonny Rollins was already playing by the Sixties, wasn't he? – this is music from the Sixties, right? She nodded. I was already playing him at the university, she said, he was one of my maestros. All right, I said, let's replay that record.

At this point, we were the only two left at the bar. The music started again, and the waiter brought over the absinthe. Tecs lit a long ivory pipe and took a couple of puffs. An Indian chief gave me this, she said, it's a good-luck pipe, the Indian was from the Arapaho tribe, near Arkansas, he told me to smoke it at difficult times. "Everything Happens to Me" started playing again. And just when the saxophone broke into an expansive phrase, Tecs grabbed my hand and said: his name was Almeida, Mr. Almeida. Good lord, I said, Portugal's full of Almeidas. Tecs gave me an encouraging smile. An Almeida from Cape Verde who was a prison guard at Caxias many years ago, she whispered, if he's still alive, it won't be that hard to track him down – you know your way around the municipal archives.

I asked her if we could let the record finish. By now I wanted to hear the song to the end. Tecs raised her glass of absinthe and invited me to toast. I had a few drops left. What should we drink to? she asked. To Sonny Rollins, I said, he deserves it. To Sonny, she said. And then she added: and to your search.

Fourth Circle. Uncle Tom.
Reboleira. Restoration.

I looked around. The bus was practically empty. Near the exit stood two black youths, their hair in corn rows, in front of me was an old woman with a shopping bag, on the long back seat, an unassuming man. I got up and walked toward the driver. A sign read: no talking to the driver. He was a very small Cape Verdean, his face indifferent. I told him I was going to Reboleira and I wanted to know the stop. He made a sound with his lips, a slight whistle. It's the end of the line, he answered, staring straight ahead, everyone gets off, Reboleira's the end of the line, and that's it.

I was the last to get off. Before me was a circular area filled with weeds, and at the center, some sort of enormous granite ball that must have been a monument to something or someone. Nearby stood a large metal plaque with the words, Welcome to Reboleira, and a map of the area, with streets and places marked. I tried to get my bearings. Rua Cabo Verde, Rua Angola, Rua. S. Tomé, Rua Moçambique. Four plain buildings facing each other, unpaved roads and squalid spaces, I turned right, walked along a narrow path bordered by struggling trees, you could tell there was no drainage or other infrastructure, at last I found Rua S. Tomé. I looked for number twenty-three; as usual, there weren't any names by the buzzer, you had to remember the floor, the sixth to the left, or the sixth to the right? I just picked one, a thick voice answered, with a slight African accent that muddied the vowels. It's Slowacki, I said, and he said: this is Almeida, come on up, sixth floor, right side, there's no elevator.

The door opened to a fat, old African woman with thinning hair. I stepped inside and found myself in a very small dining room, dirty dishes piled up on a round table. In the corner, a girl of about fifteen was ironing a great heap of laundry. My granddaughter,

Maria Osita, the woman said, make yourself comfortable, my husband will be in shortly. She had me sit down on a chair facing the dirty dishes. In front of me, on the otherwise bare wall, hung a colored print of an island with a volcano.

A man walked in, looking half-asleep, white hair rumpled. A black man, about sixty years old, with surprisingly pale eyes, almost the eyes of an albino, he was thin, in an undershirt, but his belly was swollen like a watermelon. Pleased to meet you, he said, I'm Joaquim Francisco Tomaz de Almedia, but you can call me Tom, actually, Uncle Tom, if you prefer, that's what everyone calls me. Speaking in Creole, he had the two women leave, I didn't really understand, but he clearly didn't want them underfoot. Then he went to the cupboard and took down a bottle and two shot glasses. Cachaça, he said, made in my country. I tried to decline, but he wouldn't hear of it. I took a sip; my mouth was on fire. Listen, Mr. Almeida, I said, I want to know everything. He stared at me with his pale eyes, poured himself another drink, and gulped it down. What everything? he asked. Everything, I said. Everything is nothing, he answered spreading his arms wide. If everything is nothing, then I want to know this everything that's nothing, I answered, how she died, why she swallowed glass, who turned her in, you know, you guarded her for a week at Caxias, you could talk with her, you know everything about Isabel.

He took another shot. Everything is nothing, he repeated. Mr. Almeida, you're getting drunk, I said, you're getting drunk. He lit a cigarillo. Better that way, he said, that way, there's no more fear. Fear of what? I said, listen, Mr. Almeida, I've come a long way to find out, because a friend of mine urged me to find out, and at this point, the truth is burning inside me, I have to know the truth before going back such a long distance: did Isabel kill herself because someone turned her in, and if this is why, then how'd she die, and when, and how, I want to know the truth, you mustn't fear the truth, so much time has passed, this country's changed, no one can hurt you now, tell me everything. He stared at the ceiling and murmured: everything is nothing.

I slammed my fist down on the table, and the glasses rattled. Enough! I said, enough, Mr. Almeida, or Uncle Tom, if you prefer, most of all, I want to know what made Isabel commit suicide – what were her motives – were they personal or political? I didn't know her personal motives, he answered calmly, the young lady never spoke to me of personal motives. Damn it, I said, trying to contain myself, you were her guard, you must have had a chance to look at her, you must have noticed if she was pregnant – if her belly was swollen – you had eyes, didn't you, to see her belly! Mr. Almedia stroked his eyebrows. These eyes saw nothing, he responded, serenely. Of course, I said, because nothing is everything and everything is nothing, but I'm told Isabel was pregnant, that's what I heard from one of her friends. He drank another shot and said in Creole: good cachaça. Then he put his hand over his heart and whispered: the young lady was not pregnant, this I can swear to. That surprises me, I said, but anything's possible; with Isabel, anything was possible, and so, Mr. Almeida, why did she swallow glass?

The man's wife opened the door and peeked in. Mr. Almeida waved her off without a word, and she promptly retreated. We both fell silent. Mr. Almeida relit his cigarillo that had gone out and murmured: it's all a big scam, dear sir, a big scam. And I gathered my courage and took another sip of cachaça. Tell me about this scam, Mr. Almeida, please, you're the only one who can tell me about this scam. The old man stood up and went and locked the door to the hallway, he inhaled and blew out two concentric smoke rings, which he stared at as if they were the most important thing in the world. The young lady never ate glass, he murmured, she didn't die in prison, that's just what everyone believes, but the truth's something different.

On impulse, I placed my hand on his and squeezed. If you know what the truth is, I said, Mr. Almeida, or Uncle Tom, if you prefer, then please tell me, nothing bad will happen to you. Mr. Almeida stepped over to the window and looked out. The glass was wet with rain. It was drizzling. Sometimes in the afternoon I stand at this window and look at the street, he murmured so I could barely hear, and I watch the dogs, this area's full of stray dogs, you might not understand, my friend, but these dogs tie me to Cape Verde more than anyone I know, because Cape Verde's full of stray dogs, too, and they're usually yellow dogs, just like in Reboleira, and then I start thinking about what it is that ties this country to Cape Verde, and I've come to believe it's the stray dogs, the yellow dogs, because, really, I don't have anyone left in Cape Verde, my whole family is dead, I have a cousin who's a government official, but he doesn't want to know about someone like me, a guard in a political prison during fascism, he won't even say hello, he's an asshole, he has no idea what I did for democracy in this country and in his country, how many times I risked my life, that idiot doesn't understand a thing: he's an official. And what about you? I argued, haven't you been an official your entire life as well? Yes, he murmured, but consider in what capacity, you know, dear sir, at times the prisoners arrived beaten to a pulp, because the PIDE had scooped them up, and they meant business, after the infirmary, prisoners went into the cells with their faces bruised, their lungs swollen from the beatings, and then I, Uncle Tom, looked after them, made them coffee, iced their injuries, and they confided in me, gave me letters for their families that I mailed at the main post office, things like that, I helped them, I did everything I could, because I knew what my brothers in Cape Verde were suffering to be free, they were suffering the exact same things, and then one evening, Miss Isabel arrived.

Uncle Tom paused. She didn't have any identification, he went on, and she said her name was Magda. They beat her during her interrogation, and the secret police had already struck her in the car, her face was swollen and she had bags under her eyes, who knows why she felt like my daughter, a Cape Verdean like me, is it strange what I'm saying? – a true Cape Verdean like me, even though she was blond.

Mr. Almeida grew quiet, he opened the window, leaned out, looked below, and tossed out his cigarillo butt. That's how the scam started, he added, but to be honest, I have to admit I was also paid, no, really, I did it *because* they paid me, I mean, it wasn't for ideological reasons, basically, I needed a little cash, my wife had given birth to our fourth child, and you know, dear sir, with what they pay a prison guard, I couldn't support a family of seven, including my mother, like I needed to. At least to keep food on the table. You probably know Cape Verde's national dish is cachupa, made with hominy, beans, cassava root, and beef or pork, and this is rich cachupa, but we only ate poor cachupa, with corn and a slice of blood sausage, so when they offered me that money, I thought: why not provide my family with a nice rich cachupa for a few months? And so I accepted, and got involved in the scam. Mr. Almeida, I said, this is the third time you've mentioned a scam, would you mind telling me what this scam was?

Mr. Almeida returned to his seat and lit another cigarillo. His hands were trembling slightly. I realized he was nervous. You want a little cachaça? he asked. No thanks, I said. He puffed on his cigarillo and stared me in the eye, as if this secret compromised his integrity, and whispered: a simple scam, a scam, but it wound up all right in the end. And before I had a chance to respond he continued: so this is what happened, it was January, I think it was January anyway, it was cold, and that morning they brought in a female student they'd arrested at the university, there'd been a lot of student protests that week, and the police were arresting anyone they could get their hands on, they weren't recording these arrests either, just throwing them into Caxias without questioning them or anything; in the afternoon, that girl broke a bottle and swallowed glass to kill herself, she was desperate, fragile, she'd been beaten and humiliated, I was advised and received my orders, I sounded the alarm and they came for the dead girl – it was a real mess – the authorities were afraid this would get out abroad, I opened Miss Isabel's cell and handed her an overcoat, I told her to say she was the sister of the dead girl, she knelt down by the girl on a stretcher like there was nothing to it and said she wanted to accompany her sister to Santa Maria Hospital, and you might not believe it, but no one paid any attention, they just quietly let her go, the warden wasn't there, the deputy warden was an idiot, I can't tell you how frightened he was, Miss Isabel climbed into the ambulance with her supposed sister, and at the emergency room, she calmly got out of the ambulance and went on her way like it was nothing, that's it, that was the scam.

Mr. Almeida's forehead was beaded with sweat. He'd given me his life's confession, and his eyes begged me to understand. And I understood. I completely understood this old Cape Verdean who, in his own democratic way, had entered into a scam, as he put it, so he could eat a rich cachupa with his family. Maybe it was the biggest secret of his entire life, and he'd confided it to me. I was moved, I took a tissue from my jacket and held it out to him. He dried his forehead and whispered: was there anything else you wanted to know, my friend?

I looked at him and poured myself a little more cachaça, so he'd trust me. Sure, I answered, I'd like to know who gave you the orders. The Organization, was all he said. I'm sure The Organization had a face, I said, someone, I'd like to know who. Mr. Almeida scratched his head. Do I really have to tell you? he asked. If you would, I said, it's essential, truly essential. Mr. Almeida scratched his head again. I'm not sure I should tell you, he confessed, but at this point, so much time has passed, this country's changed, so much time has passed. So tell me, I said. And Mr. Almeida, in what seemed a moment of decision, smashed his cigarillo out on a dirty plate. It was Mr. Tiago, he said, enunciating each word. And who was Mr. Tiago? I asked, where can I find him? I don't know his last name, Mr. Almeida answered, I do know he had a photography studio in Praça das Flores, he was a famous photographer, even known internationally, he photographed Alentejo, and his books were published in France, like I said, he had a studio in Praça das Flores. All right, I answered, and if he's not there now – if I can't find him? That's easy, Mr. Almeida said, just ask at the butcher shop on the corner, the butcher there knew him extremely well, and I'm pretty sure he'll know how to track him down, that butcher knows me, too, because once in a while I'll go and buy some meat for a rich cachupa, but we can't allow ourselves a rich cachupa very often, you know.

I looked at him, and he looked at me. I suppose our conversation is over, he said. I suppose it is, I answered, you know, Mr. Almeida, sometimes you sound like you're British. I can't say I know the British, he said, I'm just a Cape Verdean, or at least I was, I'm not even sure what I am anymore, I live here in the outskirts, you know, I'm most familiar with the outskirts.

I got to my feet and headed for the door. Mr. Almeida shook my hand. I stepped onto the landing and he followed me out. Goodbye, Mr. Almeida, I told him, as I took the first stair. Goodbye, he said, but I'd rather be called Uncle Tom, the mailman's the only one who calls me Mr. Almeida. Think of me as your mailman, I said, going down the stairs, but don't worry, I won't ring your buzzer a second time. He leaned over the railing and called in a low voice: you mustn't think I'm a communist, that would be a mistake, I did it for rich cachupa. But that girl was nice.

I reached that circle filled with weeds and looked around. Not even the shadow of a taxi. And why would there be one available in Reboleira? The bus I'd taken was still at the stop. A note on the dashboard read: next departure, eight o'clock. The doors were open. I climbed on board and resigned myself to the wait. It was only an hour.

Fifth Circle. Tiago. Lisbon. Image.

The tram stopped right in front of the Cister Pastry Shop. I took the opportunity to get myself a coffee. The server greeted me like he knew me. Maybe I knew him, too; I couldn't remember. I smiled and nodded and left him a tip of fifty escudos, then walked along Rua da Escola Politécnica, toward Monte Olivete. It's a cobblestone street with a sharp downward slope, a slippery street, and it was drizzling. I raised the collar of my jacket and continued downhill. I walked past the British Institute, pink and white, with its brick spires, I remembered that one of my girlfriends taught there, a sloppy girl, a bit careless but a wonder in bed, and she'd make us picnic baskets that were out of this world. Back then, you'd go to the Fonte da Telha beach, and no one was there, just the fishermen and their dogs, old yellow or rust-colored dogs. They reminded me of Mr. Almeida's dogs.

Praça das Flores was deserted. In front of a fancy restaurant – the kind with a bell you had to ring to get inside the door – a Mercedes pulled up and out stepped a man in blue and a lady in pink. I just hoped the butcher's was still open. It was still open. In that area, stores closed late. The butcher was wrapping a leg of lamb up in thin paper. I decided to take a chance and said in Spanish: *hola, buenas tardes*. The man looked at me, puzzled. He might not speak Spanish, but surely he understood it. He had a ruddy, jowly face that suited a butcher, with blue capillaries spreading over his nose. He probably ate a lot of meat. He put the leg of lamb in the refrigerator and asked me how he could be of service. Some information, I said in my bad Spanish, a simple piece of information, I'm just looking for Mr. Tiago. The butcher regarded me with a serious expression that turned to puzzlement, and then he forced himself in poor Spanish: *y quién es*? What do you mean? I said, pretending to be credulous, you know very well who he is, he's the famous photographer who had a studio around here some years back, Mr. Tiago, the photographer. He started slicing up a miniature ham and said meditatively, almost to himself: I'm taking this home for dinner, it's from Chaves, do you like ham? I obliged him by accepting a small piece, and found it quite delicious. But maybe a little spicy for my taste, too much paprika; in Spain, I said, we cure our ham beneath the snow, mountain ham, of course. Beneath the snow? he said, I've never heard of such a thing, we have snow here in the winter, too, at least up in the Serra da Estrela mountains, up north, but we never bury our ham beneath the snow, but excuse me, why do you want to find Mr. Tiago? I had a sudden inspiration. Because I'm a journalist from *País*, I said, and I want some photos, we're putting together a large feature story, in Spain. He stared at me and set his elbows on the marble countertop. I don't understand, he said evenly. *El País*, I repeated, haven't you heard of the paper *El País*, it's the most important newspaper on the Iberian peninsula. The butcher stared at me with eyes, which, at that moment, truly seemed bovine. I don't know that paper, he said, sounding annoyed, I use newspapers to wrap up meat.

The situation was growing difficult. I didn't know what else I could say. Stalling, I asked: could I have another piece of ham?

He held it out to me on a spatula, and said, well?, in a definitive manner. And right then, I had another inspiration, the kind that comes from the gods; savoring the ham in my mouth, I whispered: you know who sent me? Well, it was Mr. Almeida – or, if you prefer – Uncle Tom. And the butcher broke into a grin. Uncle Tom, he said, that poor bastard, Uncle Tom. He dried his hands on his white apron and said: why didn't you say so? Mr. Tiago moved to Rua Dom Pedro Quinto, with a view of Belvedere di S. Pedro de Alcântara, on the door, you'll find a brass plaque – he can afford one at this point – and it will read: World and Photography.

The plaque on the door was discreet, with the words *World & Photo*. I rang the bell, and the front door opened at once. The foyer seemed to be in the Manueline style, with stone vaults and a cloister of eighteenth-century azulejos. It felt like I was in the home of some painter I knew. But I was there for something important, not to dine with friends. A secretary met me, her short skirt revealing a pair of chubby legs, and she asked me what I wanted. All I said was I wanted Mr. Tiago. She asked for my name. All I said was:

Slowacki. The secretary had me wait in a small, tastefully furnished parlor with photographs on the walls that I didn't bother to look at. She told me Mr. Tiago would be busy for about another fifteen minutes with some fashion photos. I sat down, lit a cigarette, and started reading a news magazine.

Perhaps Tiago was my age, or perhaps he was a few years younger, it was hard to tell. He had a buzz cut and wore a linen jacket and an Indian foulard around his neck. He was extremely elegant, smoking a cigarette in a long ivory holder.

Good afternoon, he said, were you sent by the agency? I told him no. Sorry, he said, I was expecting a critic from an agency, someone to review my show. I put out my cigarette and stood up. No, I answered, I'm here on private business, regarding someone you met a long time ago. He looked puzzled but unfazed. Come into my studio, he said, we can speak more freely there.

He led me down a hallway that opened out to a balcony, which looked out over an enormous space with very high ceilings and granite columns. It seemed like a convent refectory, and maybe it really was at one time. We went down a small, metal staircase painted green, and he had me sit on a couch adjacent to another, at the center of this large space. All around us were tripods and cameras, backdrops of various colors, white umbrella lights. The walls were covered in small color photos I couldn't quite make out.

Well? he said and crossed his legs as he sat on the couch. Well, I said, I'm here for Isabel. He looked confused, then his expression grew more ironic. He untied the foulard around his neck and draped it over the armrest. Isabel, he said, musing, Isabel, my dear sir, I've known dozens of Isabels in my life, it's such a common name in Portugal, what Isabel do you mean – an actress, a model, or something else? Or something else, I answered. Perhaps you could explain a bit more, he said. I put on a patient look and said, I'll thoroughly explain so you can thoroughly understand, Mr. Tiago: this Isabel went by Magda, but that was only a code name, and I think you very well know both her name and her code name, let's just say she was Isabel known as Magda, the same name as another who may or may not figure into this story, now do you have something to say? His ironic expression turned back to confusion. Could you explain a bit more? he said. All right, I went on, I'll explain a bit more: many years ago, you might say, about thirty years ago, Isabel known as Magda wound up in the Caxias political prison, and you, Mr. Tiago, were in The Organization, I'm not sure if it was the underground Communist Party, or a different underground party, seeing how all parties during Salazar's dictatorship were underground, and you, well, you, Mr. Tiago, you had Isabel escape prison posing as someone else, Isabel arrived at Santa Maria Hospital and you had all trace of her disappear, but you know where those traces lead, you know something, and I want to know it, too.

The photographer shifted positions and lit another cigarette in his long ivory holder. He seemed uneasy. Silent, he eyed me from head to toe. And then he said: are you a journalist? I allowed myself a chuckle. Though I didn't want to be sarcastic, his question somehow invited sarcasm, and so I told him: you couldn't be further from the truth, Mr. Tiago, I assure you, your guess is completely off-track, death is a curve in the road, to die is simply not to be seen. Then why? he asked, even more perplexed, to what end? To make concentric circles, I said, to finally reach the center. I don't understand, he said. I'm working with colored dust, I answered, a yellow ring, a blue ring, like the Tibetan practice, and meanwhile, the circle is tightening toward the center, and I'm trying to reach that center. To what end? he asked. I lit a cigarette as well. It's simple, I answered, to reach consciousness, you photograph reality: you must know what consciousness is.

The photographer went over to what seemed to be a storage shelf. He rummaged in a box a while, then returned with some photos and held one out to me. Take a look at this picture, he said, a photo's something that watches us, pursues us, maybe; look at this baby sitting on a blanket, a bow in his hair – that's me. He paused. Now I ask myself, is this who I am? Is this who I was? Who I've been? Who was this I that I now say is Tiago and is with me every day? He held out another photo. A more recent picture this time, of a boy and girl. He smiled pensively and said, look at these two on their little bike, the girl in back is hugging the boy and leaning forward, smiling innocently for the camera, I took this picture years ago, and these were my children, and I ask myself, are they still my children? That's not possible, I tell you, and I'd like to do a better job of documenting what was, but what was? He paused again, then said: if you only realized how tricky photography becomes when it's studied by philosophers! – yet I am a photographer, I tell myself in moments of pride, and I, too, no, I *especially* have a right to my opinion, though I can't seem to manage one, because photography surpasses me, is beyond me, and then I think: do the photographs of a lifetime represent time divided among several people or one person divided into several different times?

I stared at him and smiled. My smile was friendly, though I could feel a slight irritation growing inside, like an itching of the soul. Listen, Mr. Tiago, I said, I understand your fascination with photography, it's your profession and you want to reflect on it, but it's a bit late for that, you should have started your reflecting a lot earlier, because a person must reflect a while before deciding something fundamental in his life, but you're forgiven: I too began to write before I'd reflected on what writing truly was, and maybe if I'd understood from the start I would never have written a thing, but hold on, that's not really the problem, now we've come to the real problem.

The photographer looked at me, and once again, irony seemed to flicker across his face. He held a third photo between his fingers like a poker card, but he didn't show it to me. All he said was: let me philosophize, at least on this last photo; I'm reminded that someone said the photograph is death, because it fixes the unrepeatable moment. He flipped the photo with his fingers, as if it really were a playing card, and went on: but I still ask myself: and what if it were life instead? – immanent, peremptory life that lets itself be caught in an instant, that regards us with sarcasm, because it's there, fixed, unchanging, while we instead live in variation, and then I think the photograph, like music, catches the instant we fail to catch, what we were, what we could have been, and there's no way you can counter this instant, because it's righter than we are – but right about what? – perhaps about how this river changes, as it flows and carries us along, and about the clock, about time which controls us and which we try to control. Another of his pauses, a drag of his cigarette, and he went on: life against life, life in life, life on life? Perhaps. It's a riddle I leave to you while you look at this photo.

He held out the picture and waited for my reaction. I looked, and I saw Isabel. She was wearing a long, dark overcoat that came down to her ankles. There was no expression on her face, perhaps just slight surprise. She was standing at an airport check-in counter, a very small suitcase at her feet.

The photographer stood up and asked me to join him. I'd like you to take a look at my show that's opening next week in London, he said. I began to study the photographs on the walls. They were all Polaroids of faces or landscapes. He put a finger to his lips, as if this were a secret, but I doubt that's what he meant, of course. You see, he said, I've photographed reality with my Polaroid, it's a fantastic camera I bought in the United States, the show's title is *Polaroid-Reality*. He pointed at some images. See? he said, that's the Brooklyn Bridge, that's a car accident in Manhattan, that's a black girl who overdosed, that's a malnourished boy in Ethiopia, the rest you can look at on your own. I walked around the enormous room. Very interesting, I finally said, really very interesting, He eyed me again from head to toe as though I were a statue and said: I'll take a picture of you with my Polaroid, would you like to be the final subject in my show? Absolutely, I said, let's call it a challenge, or a duel, like they used to have in the nineteenth century. Mr. Tiago had me sit on a stool, he put up a fake backdrop behind me, a seashore and a pine forest. Hold up that photo of Isabel, he told me. I held up the photo of Isabel. Don't smile, he said, I detest photographic smiles. He raised his enormous Polaroid and snapped the picture.

The camera spat out the photograph, and Tiago waved it around to dry. Then he looked at the picture and showed it to me. There was a stool, the backdrop of the sea in the distance, and the photo of Isabel in the foreground. Tiago kept staring at the picture. Where are you? he said, it's like you don't exist. Exactly, I said. Exactly what? he asked. Exactly, I answered. But where do you come from? he asked. I looked at him and smiled. From somewhere very bright, I said, so bright, sometimes the camera lens is blinded, in any case, this picture's going with me. I slipped the photo into my pocket and said: and Isabel? He held out his hand to shake. Isabel left that same night for Macao, he answered, she took a direct flight to Hong Kong, Magda sent her – the real Magda – she sent her to a Catholic priest, I believe, who was in Macao or on the island of Coloane, I can't remember, I have no idea who he was, I'm afraid, I don't know his name, it could be he's still alive, maybe you can keep tightening a circle around that person you're searching for, I don't know what else I could tell you, goodbye, sir. He walked me to the small iron staircase and shook my hand again. Sorry not to go up with you, he said, but you can easily find your way – and mind your image – one of these days, it'll stay behind in the lens.

Sixth Circle. Magda. Priest.
Macao. Communication.

T he garden lane was deserted. The old Chinese gatekeeper wore a cap with *The Grotto of Camões* written on the plastic brim.

We're closing, the gatekeeper said, I'm about to close the gates. I don't need much time, I tried with a smile, just a quick trip to the Grotto of Camões. He answered, reasonably: why go at this late hour? Come back tomorrow morning, sir, the garden will be cool, the cave will be cool, tomorrow morning you can enjoy the cool air, now all you'll find are sleeping bats. Yes, I understand, I said, but it just so happens that I really do need to visit the cave tonight: I've had an inspiration. The gatekeeper removed his cap and scratched his head. I don't understand, he said. What's your name? I asked. He gave me a timid smile. In the registry office, my name is Manuel, he answered, because in the registry office here, we have Portuguese names, but my real name, my Chinese name, is something else. He uttered a Chinese name and smiled again. And what does your name mean in Chinese? I asked. It means Light Shining Upon Water, he said. This seemed like the perfect opportunity, and I slipped my arm into his. Listen, Light Shining Upon Water, I said, I have a shining light as well, and it's this light that made me think to visit the cave this very night, look, see up there? I pointed to a bright star, the brightest in the sky. It's from there, I said, that I get my inspiration, or my idea, call it what you will. He raised his arm as I did and pointed. The stars are guides, he said, they guide everything, and we pitiful humans just don't know it. My friend, you comfort me, I said, because you understand me, you know, I got a message from that shining light, it's called Sirius. He brought his raised arm alongside mine and looked at me doubtfully. You're not familiar with the Macao sky, he said, his voice apologetic, sorry, but you're really not familiar with our sky, that star has a different name in Chinese, in Latin, it's something else, if I'm saying it correctly in your language, it's called Canopus, that star is Canopus, you're a bit confused, my friend: from these latitudes your star can't be seen; I know the sky, I've studied it. Now I, too, scratched my head. All right, I said, I'll give you that; still, I did receive a message – from Sirius or Canopus, I couldn't say – but I have to get inside that cave where that great, half-blind poet praised Christianity in the sixteenth century, and I have to get in there tonight.

He dug in his pocket and pulled out a bunch of keys. The only ones who come here are Chinese, all of them with birdcages, he said, following a logic that escaped me, they each have a little songbird in a cage and they'll get their bird to converse with their neighbor's bird, and this is how it's done in China, the birdies chatter and make friends, and so their owners also make friends, and they, too, get to talk. He paused and stared at me, looking distressed. But you don't have a birdcage, he went on, and there's no one else here with a birdcage, the only ones left in the garden are two old mahjong players who'll leave by the smaller gate, what else is there for you to do here now, except run into bats? I need to get into the cave tonight, I insisted, you know, friend, you might say it's part of my destiny, that destiny the stars steer, you yourself believe in the stars, please let me stay, I'll leave by the smaller gate, too, let me stay, please, maybe that half-blind poet of the sixteenth century will even help me out tonight, here in this garden that smells of magnolias. The gatekeeper looked at me with something like pity. This garden doesn't smell of magnolias, he replied, this garden smells of piss, because all the Chinese piss on the trees, they're too lazy to go to the bathrooms we installed near the fountain, and so this garden stinks of piss. Very well, I agreed, under the light of that star which guides my terrestrial journey, I'll remain in this garden that stinks of piss; it's true, I haven't brought any birds in a cage, but I'm here to follow a destiny which I'll eventually come to know.

The gatekeeper stepped aside and handed me a small flashlight. This should help, he said, you can leave it at the outside gate when you go. I walked down the path, breathing deeply, waiting for the stink of piss, but nothing stank, a cool breeze had risen and carried the smell of the sea. Beneath a streetlamp, two Chinese were playing mahjong, I said hello and they nodded in return. One was building superior honors, with a row of four white dragons, the other was working on a set of characters. I thought I could use both dragons and characters that night, and I headed for the cave. I was halfway down the garden path when I heard a whistle behind me from one of the players. You want to watch? he called, we don't have anyone to watch, and mahjong needs an audience. I signaled no with my hand and continued on my way; at the cave entrance I turned on the gatekeeper's flashlight.

And I simply walked in, like I would my own home. I thought I'd light a cigarette, I lit one, and just then a bat started to squeak. I caught the bat in the beam of the flashlight, in all that darkness, and the bat, squeaking, told me: hello, handsome, have you made contact?

It was Magda's voice.

Hello, I answered, I have. Where are you speaking from? the bat asked. From Macao, I answered, I'm in a cave in Macao, and what about you, Magda, where are you speaking from? Oh, the usual place, she answered, go ahead and guess. I couldn't say, I murmured. It's easy, she said, it's easier than you think, we actually met right here. Listen, Magda, I said, I'm in no mood for games, if you want to tell me, okay, otherwise, just drop it. The bat squeaked:

I'm in the Brasileira do Chiado, you big dope, I'm having a coffee granita. So when is it there? I asked. The bat let out a little ringing laugh. It's the Sixties, you big, handsome dope – and when is it that you'd like your Magda to be talking with you? I heard the clinking of glasses and silverware, and then the bat squeaked: and to what do I owe this pleasure? You can thank Sirius, I said, or maybe Canopus, I can't be sure now. You are so difficult, she said, and why are you in Macao? I'll tell you why, I answered, but I want to hear your version first, what you spread around isn't very convincing. My version of what? she asked, playing dumb. Of what happened to Isabel, I answered, you're the one who spread that story around, all the final details we have about her came from you, I want to hear the real version, in your own words.

I directed the flashlight over the walls of the cave. To my right was a bronze bust of the half-blind poet. A few stalactites hung from the ceiling. All right, the bat squeaked, so listen. I found the bat with my beam, it let go of the rock with one foot, and now dangled only by the other. I could see Magda clearly, sitting in her chair in Brasileira, calling the waiter over to order another drink, an *agua de cebada*. The waiter didn't understand, and Magda, in a condescending tone, carefully explained that it was barley water, but in Valencia, it was called *agua de cebada*, that's what the Spanish say, and it was high time the Portuguese learned this, if they wanted to call themselves Iberians. I lit another cigarette and waited.

Isabel committed suicide, the bat squeaked, this I'm sure of, she swallowed two bottles of pills, her last meal, Veronal of some kind, I can even describe the scene for you, listen: a modest room, a small pension in Campo de Ourique, a view out the window of the Estrela Basilica, she pulled back the curtains, a brilliant white moon, she covered the lamp with a blue scarf, the room turned pale blue, on the bed was a crocheted blanket, the kind found in provincial hotels, she rang for water. An ancient maid arrived. She was fat and had a visible mustache. Isabel said: I want some water, a big bottle of good water. And the maid returned with a bottle of Luso water. That's it, Isabel said and laughed, it helps people to pee, I won't need to pee anymore. It's good for people to pee, said the maid with some regret, for you, too, Miss, you seem a bit wan, that must be toxins, that must be why you're so pale, you'll see, a bottle of Luso water, that's just what you need to rid yourself of toxins and get some color back in your cheeks, like the color I had at your age, when I didn't have so much pain from my arthritis. And so Isabel opened the bottle of Luso water and swallowed four or five pills to make herself feel calmer, then she looked out at the Estrela Basilica, which was white as a cookie, no, it *was* a cookie in the Lisbon sky, so ornate, embroidered like a piece of lace, and she thought: maybe I'll say a prayer to the Madonna, a prayer I haven't prayed for a long while. Because a person getting ready for a long trip needs a viaticum, and Isabel needed a viaticum, she needed to talk to someone. But who, on that Lisbon summer night, with the moon so bright and the basilica like a cookie? Who? She asked the Veronal this, and felt calmer. Then she sat down at the small desk beside the washbasin and wrote a letter. It was a letter for me, for her friend Magda. She was saying goodbye and giving an exact account of that night, with no explanation for her reasons. All she said, in an underlined postscript, was that the light was pale blue and that she was looking out at the Estrela Basilica. And that's how Isabel passed away.

I waited a few seconds. Are you done? I asked. I'm done, the bat squeaked. Listen, Magda, I said, I have no idea why you're telling me this bullshit – what's in it for you? What on earth are you saying? she snapped, I know exactly what happened, I'm telling you the absolute truth. All right, I said, now *you* listen, I'm going to tell *you* the absolute truth, so listen up, you were a part of the antifascist network and you organized it all, Isabel took too many risks and had to go into hiding, you made sure she disappeared and then spread it around that she'd committed suicide due to romantic troubles, you even went so far as to publish her death notice in the paper and whipped up a story about a Seventh Day Adventist Mass at the Cascais Chapel, only just then, by pure coincidence, Isabel was picked up in a roundup by the secret police during a student protest, she didn't have any papers and lied about her identity, said her name was Magda, they tossed her in Caxias without even questioning her, back then, interrogations came later, but you know all this better than me, I don't know why I'm wasting my breath, one day a girl wound up in a cell, she was covered in bruises, and she swallowed glass, that girl, yes, she really did commit suicide, and you organized Isabel's escape with the help of a prison guard, and that night, you had Isabel board a plane for Macao, right here in Macao, where I happen to be at this very moment.

Silence followed. Then came Magda's voice in a whisper: how did you manage to figure it out? Easy, I answered, I dug around, did a little investigating. So if you already know everything, she said, why get ahold of me? Because I don't know everything, I said. I want to know who the Macao priest was that you sent Isabel to. She giggled. Oh, who can remember anymore, she said in a falsetto. Go on and try, I urged her. This waiter's not coming back, she said, it's been a half hour since I ordered my *agua de cebada*. Go on and try, I said, please, for once in your life, would you just show your cards? Sometimes, Magda sighed, telepathy can play such cruel jokes: you never know where you're coming from in time, where *are* you coming from in time? Way ahead of you, I answered, a lot of time has passed. Then I don't know if you'll find him, she said, if he's still alive, but his name is Father Domingos, he ran a leper colony on Coloane, that's where we sent Isabel, I'm not sure what else I can tell you.

I said: so long, Magda. I think the bat waved goodbye with its tiny foot. I turned off the flashlight and left the cave.

*

From high on the hill, you could see the lights of Macao leading down to Porto Velho. I shut the smaller gate behind me, set the flashlight on the first step, and walked down to the city center. The square was empty. Before me stood São Paulo Cathedral, just the façade, the rest had been destroyed in a fire in the eighteenth century.

I was curious and wanted to look behind the façade, but decided the body also has its rights; the body must be pardoned for its demands, especially when someone's enjoying an earthly leave.

I looked around for a restaurant. In the farthest corner of the square was a sign in Chinese with neon lettering below in English: *Portuguese food*. I headed over. The restaurant was called Antigua Lisbon/Modern Macao. It was a real hole-in-the wall; in a small display case sat a tray with the remnants of some yellowing tripe. There was an enormous ginseng root at the center of the window, and beside it a card in Portuguese that stated: *Nós pensamos na sua virilidade*: we tend to your virility. I thought I might find something European on the menu. I pushed open the door and stepped inside. The place was empty. An old Chinese woman in a white robe and slippers was hunched over on a stool. She greeted me and got to her feet, I sat down at a nasty-looking table, and she calmly, very calmly, began wiping away all the filth. Eat Cantonese or European? she asked me in Portuguese. She was chewing on something. A piece of bread, maybe, or maybe just her dentures. European, I answered, it depends on what you have. Have watercress soup and goat, she muttered wearily, only things European watercress soup and goat. Then she studied me more closely and made a strange gesture, like some sort of exorcism. What was that? I asked, what does that mean? The old woman pushed her dentures about with her tongue, realigned them, and said: you, soul in pain, full of spirits, must go to forest, ask cleansing of forest genies.

She disappeared into the kitchen and soon returned with both the soup and the goat. The goat had a side dish of pineapple and olives, which looked revolting, but I didn't make a fuss, just started eating. And it really wasn't as bad as all that. The old Chinese woman watched me very closely with an inscrutable expression.

Why forest genies? I decided to ask, I'm not generally in the woods, I don't need any forest genies. Need someone make clean again, the old woman said, look for a person, but you full of spirits, need forest genies, but maybe prefer Catholic priest lives behind Cathedral, that pig. Why do you call him a pig? I asked, is he really a pig? Not know, she answered, but all Catholics pigs, especially priests. But I need some information, I said, then added: and your forest genies can't give me this information, I'm not in contact with them, maybe the Catholic priest can give me this information.

The old woman chewed on her dentures, and spat on the floor. Not understand, she said. Some information, I said, some information about a person; like you said, I'm looking for someone. The old woman seemed angry, and I started to feel guilty. I couldn't bear that an old Chinese woman with broken dentures was angry with me, it made me feel guilty. Where come from? the old woman asked. From the Great Dog, I answered. She thought a moment, then said: good, maybe good. And then she went on: but why look for Catholic priest? I finished the last piece of pineapple and wiped my mouth with my napkin. Because need Catholic priest, I said, feeling myself growing irritated as I imitated her, you old biddy, only priest can give information I need.

The old woman took my plate and shuffled into the kitchen. When she returned, she was carrying a bottle of mandarin liqueur, and she poured me a glass and said: you drink, poor thing, you poor christ. Too true, I said, you've put your finger on it, old woman, I poor christ, but then you know who Christ was. The old woman turned her dentures over yet again and placed her hand over her heart. I half Christian half animist, she said, you Christian only, need Catholic priest who stay on square, you go out, shoo, shoo. Do you know this priest's name? I asked. Priest hear confession and cool off in square, the old Chinese woman answered. Yes, yes, I said, but his name – what's his name? He no like animists like me, she went on with her own logic, and I no like him. And what does this priest do? I asked. First he heal lepers on Coloane, the old woman said, but now no more lepers, he unemployed and sit on chair in square and cool off.

I drank a glass of that sickeningly sweet mandarin liqueur, paid, and went out to the square.

I walked around the façade of the cathedral and saw the priest. He was sitting on a chair, cooling off. I went over and said good evening. He offered me the small chair he was using as a foot stool.

He was an old, portly priest who looked vaguely oriental, no doubt a mix of Portuguese and Chinese. But his complexion seemed somewhat olive, or perhaps that was the yellowish cast of the neon lights off the façade, which reflected back as violet. His frock was rolled up a bit over his crossed legs, and he wasn't wearing any pants, so I saw his fleshy, hairless calves.

My son, he said, did you wish to confess? I sat down and replied: maybe it's a bit too late; by now, I think it's a bit too late. Puffing on his fat cigar, he said: it's never too late to confess. But I've finished everything I had to finish, I answered, and I have my own little corner in the universe. He took a giant puff on his cigar and blew smoke in my face. He carefully scratched his calves and said: the universe is vast, but you're here, in this little corner of the world, and it's never too late, man of mud. I've lost all my mud, I explained, I've become pure light. He scratched his calves. What do you mean, he murmured. Think of me as a pulsar, I said, I'm not sure I'm being very clear. Is that some kind of forest genie? he asked, are you by any chance an animist? No, I said, you might say what I'm talking about sends bursts of light over every wavelength; you know what, Father, it's a matter of neutrons. This all reeks of animism, the priest said, so do you want to confess or not?

The situation was growing difficult. But at this point, I was used to encountering difficult situations. I studied him some more, and he suddenly looked younger: the light off the square made his skin seem smooth and unlined. Are you Catholic? he asked. I'm everything you want, I said, I was baptized by Roman Apostolic Christian parents when I was seven days old. The priest puffed on his huge cigar again, and this time he spared me and blew his smoke into the air. He seemed to be thinking. He thought a while, scratched himself, and asked: my son, how long since your last confession? Forever, I replied, forever. He grew meditative. Do you mean to say you've never confessed in your entire life? he asked. That's right, I said, I never confessed in my entire life. And then I added: but I could confess tonight, seeing that tomorrow is my birthday. Tomorrow's the fall equinox, the priest said, that's not promising, there's madness on that day, the tides rise. Sorry, I said, but are you a priest or a fortune-teller? Excuse me, but since I've agreed to confess, let me confess, and we'll be done with it. Confess your sin, my son, he said and scratched at his calves. Listen, Father, I said, could you stop your scratching, your scratching's interfering with my concentration, not to mention my contrition. You have to say that you repent with all your heart, the priest said. I repent with all my heart, I whispered. Say it again, he told me, I didn't hear you. I repent with all my heart, I said again, louder. The priest rolled his frock back down. Confess your sins, he said. All right, I said, it's a long story, so I'll be brief, because I like the idea of being brief on this night in Macao, on the eve of the fall equinox, so here goes: I too have made the tides rise, that is my sin. That seems a bit vague, my son, the priest replied, you have to be more specific. I wrote books, I whispered, that is my sin. Were they dirty books? the priest asked. What do you mean, dirty? I said, there was nothing dirty, just a sort of arrogance toward reality. The priest puffed on his cigar. Excuse me, Father, I said, but could you stop blowing smoke in my face? It breaks my concentration. He blew his smoke in the air and said: arrogance, according to the precepts of the Mother Church, arrogance is pride, you're guilty of the sin of pride, but you have to be more specific. You see, I said, at a certain point, I got it into my head that the stories I imagined could recur in reality, and I was writing stories that were evil – that's the word – and then much to my surprise that evil really did recur in reality, and so, I've steered events, this is my pride. And? the priest asked. And what? I asked in turn. And all the other sins you've committed in your life, he said, who knows what other sins you must have committed in your life. A bunch, I said, but they don't matter, they're just a part of man's miseries, I don't give a damn about them, let's not bother with them. Around here, pardons aren't just dished out like soup to the poor, the priest said, first you confess, then you're pardoned, that's the rule.

I looked at him and started feeling slightly queasy, like I'd been feeling ever since I got down here. Trying to keep calm, I thought it had to be the old Chinese woman's goat with pineapple. Father, listen, I said, if you don't give me absolution, so be it, at this point, I really don't give a damn, but I would like to know one thing: did you take care of lepers on Coloane a long time ago? He stared at me, stunned. Coloane, he said, sure, Coloane, those were wonderful times, there were so many lepers back then. He sighed wistfully. There were so many lepers back then, he went on, but not anymore, in Macao everyone's well, they've all become businessmen, but back then they'd arrive at the clinic with purplish hands, even missing two or three fingers, they depended on us; and to be taken care of and to stay in the clinic, they were only too happy to be baptized, they even abandoned their animism, those were wonderful times. He sighed again and went on: now there aren't even fishermen left in Macao, they buy their fish in Hong Kong.

I asked him for a cigar, which he gave me. I lit it and said: listen, Father, do you know a Father Domingos? He sighed again and whispered: Father Domingos was a saint. Concerned, I said: what do you mean *was*? – is he gone? Died six years ago, the priest said, he was a real saint. Please tell me about him, I said. Well, the priest said, finally stubbing his cigar out on the ground, Father Domingos's real name was Domenico, he came from Italy, from Sicily, before he lived in China, and he managed to get through the communist revolution with some difficulty, then I believe he arrived in Macao during the war, I was just a boy then, and he founded a leprosy clinic on Coloane, I went to lend a hand in the Fifties, I wasn't a priest yet but I was about to take holy orders. And then? I asked. And then we spent many years together, he said, we had around a hundred patients, but he was busy with various matters, he helped everyone. Everyone? I asked, Isabel, too? He seemed to reflect for a moment. Never met her, he answered. Magda, then, I said, maybe she was named Magda. So which is it, my son, Isabel or Magda? He sounded exasperated. I pulled Tiago's photo from my pocket, the one with the photo of Isabel; the priest lit a match to see, and also to light another cigar. He studied the photo a bit and then said with confidence: I don't know her, I don't know this person. Think hard, I said, her name was Isabel but she might have gone by Magda, she came from Portugal, she was a political refugee. The priest lit another match and went back to studying the photo. Sorry, he said, but I don't know her, I've never seen her. And then he went on: only Father Domingos concerned himself with these things, I just didn't have the capacity, but my son, why are you looking for her, and to what end, after all this time?

I took a big puff on my cigar and tried not to blow my smoke into his face like he was doing to me. I said, dear Father, it would take too long to tell you the whole story, I asked you to think of me as a pulsar, but I'm also a receiver, because I come from a place where splendor reigns, and I can't leave this whole area of my life in darkness. What do you mean by splendor? the priest asked. Just splendor, I said. When I was studying at seminary, they talked about the Zohar, the priest said, are you perhaps referring to that? You can think what you want, I answered, but I need to learn more about Isabel, or Magda, if that's what she went by. The priest apologized and scratched his calves. Be patient, my son, he said, I don't know if this is just a bad habit or if it's erysipelas that's bothering me, anyway, listen, I'm not an animist but I've met a lot of them, now you're forcing me to tell you things I shouldn't, but if I were you, I'd ask an animist, I don't like animists, all those spirits, when it comes to spirits, I only believe in one, even if it is a trinity, I learned this in seminary, but they have spirits for everything, a flower, a tree, a person, a picture, and if you show them your photo, they'll tell you something. All right, I said, but who can I go to? Many years ago, there was a poet here, the priest said, maybe he was an animist, maybe not, anyway, he was in touch with ghosts, too bad you never met him, in my opinion he was crazy, most of all, he smoked opium, he was a very good talker when he smoked opium, like I said, he was a poet, and maybe he could give you some information about that person you're looking for, also, I think, because he, like you, is from outside of time. And who was this person? I asked. A skeleton of sorts, the priest answered, he had a long beard and always dressed in white and sometimes, when the mood struck him, he'd go out wearing only a sheet. And what was his name? I asked. I don't know his real name, the priest said, but everyone around here called him The Ghost Who Walks, I think he lived on Avenida da Boa Vista.

I got up to leave. I said: thank you, Father, this conversation has been quite helpful. The square looked surreal, with that pretend façade and the neon lights. It reminded me of when I used to like the old avant-garde movements and imitated surrealism. I really didn't know anything back then.

I'd already gone a fair distance when I heard the priest's voice booming across the deserted square. My son, he called, I want to tell you that I pardon you. Thank you, Father, I whispered to myself. And I went on my way.

Seventh Circle. Ghost Who Walks.
Macao. Worldliness.

I t was a suffocating morning, the sun pale with humidity. A tropical storm seemed imminent. Along Porto Velho stood a line of hackney coaches. I climbed inside the first. The coach man was Chinese with a long, drooping mustache and a jaunty, tilted cap. He was sweating in his filthy frock coat. He looked at me suspiciously, perhaps because I was wearing a white shirt that came down to my hips and leather sandals. He said something I didn't understand, probably in Cantonese.

Listen, friend, I said in Portuguese, take me to the poet dressed in white, he lives on Boa Vista. Don't know, he said, in broken Portuguese. I settled back on the seat and said: the poet with the long beard. Don't know, he answered, sounding distressed. He lives on the Boa Vista promenade, I repeated, a poet, a gentleman always dressed in white. Don't know, he said, even more distressed. Listen, old fellow, I said, enunciating my words, everyone in Macao knows that poet, every last one of you, he's European, has a beard, lives with a Chinese woman, and is always dressed in white, the Chinese call him The Ghost Who Walks. Ah, he said with an enormous grin, The Ghost Who Walks, of course, Avenida da Boa Vista, he's something else in Cantonese, but I'm sure that's him, I know where to take you, trust me.

It was a wood cottage on the Avenida by the sea. There was a cane mat on the porch. Three steps led up to a shuttered door. I knocked. No one answered, and I knocked again. I waited, calm and hopeful. After a few minutes, the door opened partway, to a Chinese woman, about thirty years old. She was beautiful, elegant, in a blue embroidered jacket that came down to her knees, her hair was gathered in a bun and her eyes were dark with makeup. Good afternoon, I said, I'd like to see the master poet, I sent a card announcing my visit, I hope that he might receive me. Who are you, sir? the Chinese woman asked. My name is Slowacki, I said, but you can also call me Waclaw, I too know something about poetry. The Chinese woman opened the shutter door and had me come inside. I found myself in a living room with a wood floor and bamboo furniture, the walls were lined with cane. The master poet is resting now, the Chinese woman said, he's taken opium. All right, I said, perhaps I could speak with his wife. The Chinese woman had me sit down on a chaise-longue. I am his wife, she said, and I'm not his wife, I am his concubine, my name is Ngan-Yen, which in your tongue means Silver Eagle, may I bring you a mandarin liqueur? I agreed to a mandarin liqueur. Silver Eagle was swift and silent. She served me that unbearable liqueur I already knew, thick and sickeningly sweet, and then she clapped her hands. A Chinese servant appeared wearing a sort of coverall and cloth shoes. Fan the gentleman, Silver Eagle ordered, he's hot. The Chinese servant began to pump a bellows at the ceiling, causing the linen ceiling fan to move. I felt a little breeze and was more comfortable. Madam Ngan-Yen, I said, will I have to wait very long? She nodded in a manner I couldn't decipher. I'll go wake him, she said, the time of opium must have passed for the master poet my husband; when I open the door, you may go into his bedroom.

The Chinese woman opened the door, a bamboo shutter; I timidly stepped in and saw a man lying on the bed, covered by a white sheet. He had a long dark beard, his face was gaunt and his eyes were barely open.

To what do I owe the pleasure of this visit? he whispered. I'm not exactly sure, I stammered, they told me that in this dream we're both passing through, you might be able to give me some information about a person that you unfortunately don't know, because she was born many years after you, but you, in your infinite wisdom, might be able to tell me where to find her. He let out a weak sigh and clapped his hands, the Chinese servant rushed in and the poet gave him a nod. The servant started working a set of foot levers that operated a cloth fanning device. Where are you from? the poet asked me. He looked like a dead Christ. His face was hollow, his eyes, sunken. I'm from endless time, I answered, from the endless time that outstrips us both, you, living in this now of yours, and I who lived in my then, you, writing your poetry, and I who wrote my poetry, not as beautiful as yours, mind you, simpler, without the personal tragedies of yours. There's no personal tragedy in my poetry, he whispered, it's the story of my generation, a period transformed into poetry. Of course, I said, but you never assumed this responsibility, and why do you live at the ends of the earth, in this remote province, and direct your poetic messages at Europe – why do that?

The poet stood up. He was naked, emaciated. He pulled the sheet around him like a Roman Senator and cried out: who soiled, who tore the linen sheets I wished to die in – my chaste sheets?

He wrapped himself up to the neck in the sheet, walked to the middle of the room and went on: that small garden that was mine, who tore down the tall sunflowers, who tossed them in the street?

I stared at him. He looked like a scarecrow. He made me think of one of those awful photos from the Second World War, and I told him: Master, you remind me of a survivor, a prisoner, which probably means nothing to you, it's not important. I don't know what you're talking about, he answered, I don't know anything about anything, not the past, not the future, my poetry concerns the eternally inherent. He rang a silver bell and his concubine entered the room. We need two pipes, he said, bring them. And now, he said, tell me what it is that you want from me, but before you do, you must think carefully, you must enjoy a bowl of opium.

The servant came in with two pipes. He heated the bowls, checked the water, prepared the potion. I slowly smoked mine, afraid of losing my wits. I said: I'm looking for Isabel, perhaps you know where I might learn something about Isabel, I'm making concentric circles, like the concentric circles squeezing my brain at this very moment. The Ghost Who Walks took a long pull from his pipe. Isabel, he said, there might be an Isabel in my poetry, or in my thoughts, they're one and the same, but whether she's in my poetry or in my thoughts, she's a shadow who belongs to literature, why are you looking for a shadow who belongs to literature? Perhaps to make her real, I answered weakly, to give some meaning to her life, and to my rest.

He rose from his pallet, draped his sheet around his shoulders again, took another pull of opium, and said: listen, kindred spirit, we've crossed over time, poetry does that and more, as does opium, all I can do is make up poems, poems about mountains, for instance, mountains I've never seen, and would have loved to see during my time in Coimbra; in its way, this is a clue, but that will be up to you, to find the place and the people; if you're making concentric circles, it's up to your impulse, your imagination, to form these circles, I never wrote the poems I have in my heart, and I might never write them, but I could make them up right here, if you like.

He was quiet now and drew a deep breath. Then he closed his eyes and seemed to fall asleep. After a few minutes, I started to feel extremely embarrassed. I stood, cleared my throat, sat back down. Master, I said softly, Master, listen to me. He showed no sign of life. His eyes were closed and his thin chest didn't rise, he didn't seem to be breathing. Master, I begged, the poems.

And then he jumped up, in all his emaciated nakedness, pulled the sheet around him, and bolted to the middle of the room, eyes possessed, as if death had come knocking, and he uttered these words: when will the embrasure shutters rise once more on the ruined castle, when will the edict come and the standards wave in the cold morning breeze?

He paused, then went on in a low voice: all you need to do is find the castle. Like in a fairy tale, I said, excuse me, Master, but the mountains are full of castles. He stared straight ahead, at nothing. You have to look in the country of William Tell, he murmured. And he was quiet again.

The situation seemed to have reached a full stop. The poet's eyes bulged, staring straight ahead; his face was frightening. I wanted to ask him more, but didn't dare, and so kept quiet. And then The Ghost Who Walks whispered in a voice as from the grave: there, you'll find a man who won't expect your visit, a holy man from India, I can't make out his name, but you might guess it, if you search your life's memories, the castle is a place of meditation, dedicated to a German writer who deeply loved my Orient.

He opened his sheet again, showing his terribly thin chest, and he leaned on a Chinese chest of drawers and said: I'll die tomorrow at dawn, you arrived just in time, Mr. Waclaw.

He rang the silver bell, and his concubine appeared at once. Ngan-Yen, he whispered, see the gentleman out. He lay back down on the pallet and returned to his delirium. I followed the Chinese woman to the door, she carefully closed the woven shutter behind her, bowed to me, whispered something incomprehensible in Cantonese and then, in Portuguese, she said: safe travels. Thank you, I replied.

The coach driver was waiting out front. I climbed in and told him to take me to Porto Velho.

Eighth Circle. Lise. Xavier.
Swiss Alps. Expansion.

G ood evening, I said, I'm Slowacki. Good evening, the woman said, I'm Lise, please, why don't you join me, there's no one here, and I don't like eating alone.

I sat down. The room was enormous and poorly lit. Toward the back, a weak flame was flickering from some kind of brazier above a high-backed chair. An enlarged photo dominated the main wall, a picture of Herman Hesse in a spotless panama hat. An exotic music I couldn't make sense of was playing softly over an invisible intercom.

What is that music? I said. Lise smiled. The difficulty in Indian music, she said, lies mainly in the harmony, for us westerners, it has two basic elements, the Tala and the Raga, this is music from the Northeast that's used in traditional Manipuri dances, it's a ritual music. You certainly know a lot about India, I said, while I don't know a thing, I'm not familiar with Indian culture, it does feel strange, though, to find India here in the Swiss Alps. You get used to it, Lise said, it's not as strange as you might think, you'll see, in a little while, some music from Kerala will start playing, a Kathakali rhythm, and that's how it goes all night, they always play the same tape, I know it by heart now. Have you been here long? I asked. Almost a month, she answered. That seems long, I said, at least it would be for me, I feel like I'm in a monastery, I've never liked monasteries, it's all their rules, you see, eating so early, for instance – it's unbearable. Rules are useful when the boundaries are lost, she answered, plus there's a practical side: in the evenings, there's meditation with the Lama, and when that's done, it's good to go back to your own room and continue meditating in private. What do you mean when you say the boundaries are lost? I asked, I don't understand. If we keep talking, you'll understand, Lise said, but for now, you should decide what to eat. I opened my menu and studied it. There wasn't an item I recognized, I looked at my table companion and said: excuse me, Lise, but tonight I'm appointing you my guide, I don't know any of these dishes. She smiled again. Her smile was strange, distant, as if she were here and, at the same time, far away. They're all Indian, she said, you can trust me, I'm well-versed in India's traditions and foods. Then what would you recommend? I said. She began to read the menu. Tonight we have a wide variety of dishes, she said, from all over India, an embarrassment of riches. You decide, I said. She looked up and smiled again. I found her smile unsettling; I couldn't read it. All right, she said, to start with, I'd recommend a Thali, a light vegetarian dish typical of Southern India, vegetables cooked in curry, and papadums, you know, that fried flat bread that's very light?, and an order of spicy rice, I think that will be perfect to start with. Trying to decide on the next dish, she ran her finger down the menu. And for your second course, I recommend the Gushtaba, that's one of my favorites, it comes from Kashmir. Could you describe it? I asked. Simple, she said, it's a simple dish, spicy meatballs, lamb, usually, cooked in a yogurt sauce, a traditional dish that's eaten all over northern India. I agreed on her choices, and she called the waitress over, an olive-skinned girl dressed in a violet sari.

The music changed. I heard an odd, stringed instrument now, tambourines, and in the background, a singsong voice and what sounded like a nursery rhyme. What do you mean by losing the boundaries? I asked, excuse me, Lise, I'd like to know. She smiled her distant smile. It means the universe has no boundaries, she answered, that's what it means, and that's why I'm here, because I too have lost my boundaries. She sipped her tea that the waitress had brought. I sipped mine as well. It was a green tea, very fragrant, jasmine-scented. And so? I said. She looked at me with her vague smile and asked: do you know how many stars there are in our galaxy? I have an idea, I said, do you know? About four-hundred billion, Lise answered, but in the universe we know, there are hundreds of billions of galaxies, the universe has no boundaries. Excuse me, Lise, I said, but how do you know all these things? She stared into empty space, and said: I'm an astrophysicist, or at least I was.

Now I heard pipe music playing over the intercom, piercing notes that were almost unbearable, yet at times, were also moving. I glanced at the portrait of Herman Hess, and he too seemed to be smiling a distant smile.

Lise lit an Indian cigarillo, the very fragrant kind rolled from a single tobacco leaf. Many years ago I had a son, she said as though she were speaking past me, to the empty space she seemed to have before her; and life, she said, took him away from me. I stayed quiet, I took one of her cigarillos, the brand was Ganesh, I noticed, with an elephant god on the package. I stayed quiet, and waited for her to go on. His name was Pierre, she went on, and nature was cruel to him, hadn't allowed him certain mental faculties, but he had his own kind of intelligence, you just needed to understand it, and I did. She paused, then said: I loved him like you can love your own child, do you know how you can love your own child? Unfortunately, I never had children, I answered, but maybe you could tell me. More than yourself, Lise said, much more than yourself, that's how you can love your own children. She set her tea down. What would you say to a glass of champagne? she asked, tonight I could really go for a glass of champagne while we wait for our Thali.

I waved to the waitress who came over at once. The room was eerie. Someone had turned up the flame in the brazier, and red flickered over the portrait of Herman Hesse. Through the large windows, you could see the snowy mountaintops, the Indian music was now calling softly, like an invocation.

This music sounds like a lament, I observed. The Indians really understand the lament, she said, and they reflect this in their art, when it comes down to it, this is my lament, my invocation, though our western parameters make sure I express myself in human words. We raised our glasses in a toast of sorts. Go on, Lise, I said. He had his own kind of intelligence, she went on, and I studied and understood it; for instance, we'd found a code, one of those codes that schools for boys like my Pierre don't teach, but that a mother can invent with her son, tapping a spoon against a glass, for instance, I'm not sure I'm making myself clear, tapping a spoon against a glass. Would you mind going into a bit more detail? I said. Well, Lise said, you have to study the frequency and intensity of the message, and I understood frequencies and intensity, from my profession, from studying the stars in the Paris Astronomical Observatory, but that didn't really guide me, it was because I was his mother, because you love your child more than yourself. I understand, I said, and so? Our code functioned perfectly, she went on, we'd learned a language humans don't know, he knew how to tell me, Mama I love you, I knew how to answer, Pierre, you're my whole life, and then simpler things, too, daily things, what he needed, if he was happy or unhappy, because I have to tell you, nature may have been cruel to them, but these people, just like us, know what it means to be happy or unhappy, to feel sadness, regret, joy, everything we feel, we proud miserable beings who think of ourselves as normal. She finished her champagne, we started eating, and she went on: I don't know why I'm telling you all this – I don't even remember your name. Slowacki, I repeated, my name's Slowacki. All right, Mr. Slowacki, Lise said, one day, life stole my boy from me, because life's not just cruel, it's evil. She stared again into empty space, as if no one was sitting across from her. What would you have done? she asked. I don't know, I answered, it's really hard to answer a question like that, what did you do? Lise let out a small sigh. During the day, I wandered around Paris, she said, I'd look in store windows, at dressed-up individuals walking around, at people sitting on park benches, I'd walk by Café de Flore, stare at the people talking together at their small tables, and I asked myself why, here on planet Earth, why was there a life fashioned in such a way that I didn't understand,

I'm not sure I'm making myself clear, it all seemed like a puppet theater, I spent my nights at the Observatory, but those telescopes weren't enough for me anymore, I needed to observe vast interstellar spaces, I was here on Earth, I was a minuscule dot that wanted to study the boundaries of the universe, that's what I wanted, it was the only thing that might give me a little peace, and you, what would you have done in my place? I don't know, I answered, you're asking tough questions tonight, Lise, what did you do? Well, she said, I learned that in Chile, in the Andes, there's an observatory that's the highest observatory in the world, one of the most well-equipped, by the way, but mainly, it's the highest, and I wanted to go as high as possible, I wanted to cut myself off from this miserable earthly crust where life is vicious, I wanted to be as close as possible to the sky, so I sent off my résumé, they responded that they needed an astrophysicist like me, and I left, left France, left everything, I just brought along a small backpack full of books and a fur-lined coat, and I arrived at the highest observatory in the world. She stopped. Not much longer until the Lama's lecture, she said. Please go on, I said. She went on. I asked them if I could work on the radio telescope, she whispered, I wanted to study extragalactic nebulae, do you know what the Andromeda Nebula is? Tell me, I said. Well, Lise went on, the Andromeda Nebula is a spiral system similar to the Milky Way, however it seems tilted, so the spiral arms aren't completely visible, up to the early part of this century it wasn't certain that it was outside the Milky Way, this problem was solved by Hubble on a telescope in 1923, when he studied the Triangle Constellation, these are the boundaries of our system, and I wanted to move toward the boundaries of the Universe.

She grew quiet. The music had stopped. There was an unnatural silence in the room, as though we were outside of time. I could tell Lise wanted to go on, and I wanted to encourage her to go on, but I also didn't want to speak and break the spell. I just nodded slightly, and she said: I was at the radio telescope researching galactic radio emissions and modulated signals from possible intelligent beings, and I was sending modulated signals myself, ah, you can't imagine what it's like to be up in the highest mountains in the world, with only raging snow outside, and to send off messages to the Andromeda Nebula. Maybe I can imagine it, I replied, even if I don't have your experience. There were three of us in that position, Lise went on, a Japanese astronomer, a Chilean physicist, and I, and then two attendants who saw to our needs, and one night, one terribly snowy night, with ice crusting over the glass of the Observatory dome, I suddenly had an idea, an absurd idea, and I don't know why I'm telling you this. Tell me, Lise, I said, I'd like you to tell me. It was an absolutely crazy idea, she said, I was sending modulated messages, and I tried a modulation that held a special place in my heart, I selected a code that was dear to me, I translated it into its mathematical modulation, and I sent it. She smiled her absent smile and repeated: it was crazy. Please, Lise, I said, please go on. Well, she said, the fact of the matter is this: you might not realize it, but to send a message to the Andromeda Nebula, counting light years, it would take a hundred of our calendar years, so, a century, and to get an eventual response would take another hundred years, another century; perhaps some future astronomer might receive the eventual response to the bizarre message I'd sent, someone who didn't know me and knew nothing about me. She stopped, and this time she looked me in the eye and said: this is ridiculous, you must think I'm insane. Not at all, Lise, I assured her, I believe anything can happen in the universe, please go on. That night, she went on, there was a snowstorm, ice was building up on the glass, I stood in front of the radio telescope, not moving, feeling like I'd committed an absurdity, and just then, a message arrived from Andromeda, a modulated message, I ran it through the decoder and recognized it at once; there, in mathematical terms, but with the same frequency, the same intensity, was a message I'd heard for fifteen years of my life. She stopped and asked: do I seem crazy? You don't seem the least bit crazy, I replied, it's the universe that's crazy. Well, she went on, I was afraid my colleagues would think I was crazy, I couldn't lay it out for them in rational terms, I didn't even show them the message – how could I explain it? – a few days later, I fled the Observatory, I roamed the world, reached India, and stayed a long while, and there, in a sacred text, I discovered that the cardinal points can be infinite or nonexistent, as in a circle; it was a disturbing find, because what's left to an astronomer if you take away the cardinal points? So I started to study Indian philosophy and a theory which held that the man who's lost his way needs to symbolize the universe with an integrative art form, in short, he needs his cardinal points, and that's why I'm here, a person can't believe it's possible to reach the boundaries of the universe, because the universe has no boundaries.

She stopped, and smiled her tired smile. And what about you, she asked, why are you here? I'm trying to reach a center, I answered, I've passed through many concentric circles and I'm looking for a clue, that's why I came here. You believe in concentric circles? Lise asked. I don't know, I said, it's a practice like any other, maybe it's an integrative art form, too, but I'm not a follower. Then what are you? she asked. Just think of me as someone who searches, I answered, you know, the important thing is to search. I agree, she said, the important thing is to search, and not whether you find something or you don't.

The conference room, the sign in English indicated, was on the second floor. At the top of the stairs, I was met by a small Asian woman wrapped in a sari and holding a list. She pressed her hands together in greeting, bowed her head, and asked: what is your name, sir? Slowacki, I answered. She consulted her list and made an x with her pen. Please go in, she said.

It was an enormous room, poorly lit, with a light wood floor. The walls were bare, whitewashed. I saw Lise sitting on the floor; she was draped in an orange cloth. On the other side of the room was a wooden throne chair where the Lama would presumably sit. I walked around the room and left a card on the footstool to this chair. I signed Tadeus and wrote: room twenty-three. Then I went back to my room.

Strange that you just popped up out of nowhere, he said.

He had me sit down in the small armchair by the window while he sat in an inlaid throne chair next to the writing desk.

I'd put my western clothes back on, but I was still barefoot. You also popped up out of nowhere, dear Mr. Xavier, I said. I'm not Xavier anymore, he said, I left that name behind in the world. Yes, I went on, you truly popped up out of nowhere, I'd heard that you vanished into India, someone told me this a few years back, but here you are instead, in the Swiss Alps, playing the holy man. Please respect my beliefs, he said. Oh, sure, I said, but I think your religion also teaches you to respect the beliefs of others, I too have my convictions, in my own way, I might not call them beliefs, let's just say I have a commitment to myself. But who are you? he asked, staring at me. It's written there on the card, I answered, I'm Tadeus. I don't know you, he replied. But you did know Isabel, I said, and that's why you invited me to your suite, the name Isabel has piqued your curiosity. Isabel belongs to the past, he answered. That could be, I said, but I'm here to reconstruct that past, I'm making a mandala. Come again? he said. Just that, I answered, of course you understand what a mandala is, let's say that mine, in its way, is a type of mandala, only the rings are growing tighter, I've designed them, or better, I've passed through them, one by one, it's a strange picture, you know, the picture coming out, but I'm squeezing closer to the center. Who told you I was here? he asked. A poet, I answered, well, the ghost of a poet. You're speaking in code, Xavier said. You, too, I said, you're being rather evasive, like you're afraid to confess something. I have nothing to confess, he said. And then he went on: besides, I don't see why I have to tell you anything, when I don't even know you, about someone I met when I used to be part of the world. It's simple, I said, it's because Isabel told you about me. He grew quiet and stared off at the mountains. You want to swear Isabel never told you anything about me? I said. I don't swear to strangers, he answered, besides, swearing's not permitted in my religion. There was a strange, elusive light in his eyes, like some sort of code of silence, like he was trying to erase a promise or a memory. I wanted to call him Mr. Lama but didn't dare; I had to check my normal arrogance. I said: listen, Xavier, you can tell me something about her, you know something about Isabel, or you found out something, help me reach my center. He took a piece of paper off the table and started drawing with some colored pencils. I watched in silence. I let him go. He took about fifteen minutes. Then he handed the drawing to me. It was a double circle and beneath it were the words: "Partenope: I wander distracted and abandoned." Inside this double circle, he'd drawn the various phases of the moon and at the center, a moon with a big, round face, like in primitive drawings, the moon was orange-red. I said: Partenope – what's that mean? He looked at me, and his expression felt ironic. Now Partenope holds me, he said, like on the epitaph. I said: Partenope is Naples, that's in Italy, what was Isabel doing in Italy, excuse me, Mr. Lama, but that seems odd.

He adjusted the colored cloth draped around his shoulders. He smiled at me with an ineffable smile and murmured: we had ties with Naples. All right, I answered, but who do I need to look for, who should I contact? He stared out the window. Night was falling. I thought I heard the lowing of a cow, and everything seemed absurd. Mandalas must be interpreted, he said knowingly, otherwise, it's too easy to search for the center, study the center, look at the moon I drew, interpret it as you will, I hope you let your feelings guide you, and remember one thing: the line I wrote is a password, or at least it was back then, you too wander distracted and abandoned, and now, please excuse me, my meditation awaits.

He opened his door, and I stepped into the hall without even time to say goodbye.

Ninth Circle. Isabel. Riviera Station.
Realization. Return.

The small station was deserted at that hour. I stepped outside, to a little garden with two palm trees and two park benches surrounded by a fragrant pittosporum hedge. You could sense the sea beyond. The ground was sand and sea pebbles. It was exactly how I always imagined a small Riviera station would be. A train went by at full-speed. Direct from France, no doubt, and France lay beyond the lights of the gulf. I sat on a bench, deciding what to do next. Should I walk down the short slope and look for Via Oberdan? The garden lamps were lit. I sat on a wooden bench, right beneath a palm tree, and looked up. The moon was in its last quarter, and white as milk. I looked to another part of the sky and saw a star that was dear to me. I stretched my legs, rested my head against the back of the bench, and kept staring at the sky.

Music rose from below, sailing up over the hedge. I knew it, a Beethoven tune, *Les Adieux, L'Absence, Le Retour*.

I saw a strange individual coming toward me. He wore a rumpled tailcoat and a white top hat, and had a violin on his shoulder. He was barefoot. He stopped in front of me and doffed his hat. Good evening, he said, and welcome to this small Riviera station where you might have dreamed you'd arrive one day. He asked my permission and sat down beside me. Excuse me, he said, but don't bother looking for Via Oberdan, it's not called that anymore, now it's Via del Lavoratori del Mare. I looked at him, questioningly, and he sighed. And the print shop you're looking for, that's closed now, too, closed up years ago, replaced by an elegant pastry shop now – Bignè. I'm looking for the Social Print Shop, I said, that's what I'm looking for. He smiled and sighed again. Exactly, he answered, The Social Print Shop, the glorious Social Print Shop, destroyed by a bomb years ago, they never found the culprits, there were clues, investigations, even the shadow of a trial, and so, after

—131—

all the machinery was blown up, and after all that time those gutted rooms were left standing, someone bought the place and put in a pastry shop, where you can eat magnificent desserts. Excuse me, I said, but what did the Social Print Shop print? He sighed again. It was an anarchist print shop, he said, it printed the last leaflets of the few surviving anarchists, cheap pamphlets, and the writings of Pietro Gori, the history of the Italian anarchists; but, he sighed again, sometimes he printed wedding invitations, too, you have to survive, right?, and old man God-you're-boring had to survive. And who was Mr. God-you're-boring? I asked. The last survivor of the glorious Social Print Shop, said the man with the violin, who blew up along with his machinery. The man with the violin sighed again. Excuse me, he said, I can't seem to catch my breath, it was a steep climb, what with playing the violin. Curious, I looked at him. He ran his feet ecstatically through the sand, he'd set his violin between us on the bench. I'm amazed you know all this, I said, believe me, I'm simply amazed. Oh, please, he said, I know your entire journey, I've been following you ever since you arrived, no, in a way, I directed the entire score, consider me your orchestra director. He took out a cigarette butt and lit it. Want one?

he asked. I told him no, then said: I'd be curious to hear about this journey of mine that you say you know so well. He smiled, looked up at the sky, and said: I'll go over your trip to your last station – we won't worry about the others – your last, well, next to last, because this is the last. He took a drag of his cigarette butt and said: so, you arrived in Naples and fell into the worst sort of story, come on, that's not what we expected with that nose you have for sniffing things out, you've shown yourself to be a top-notch investigator, going to the Luna Rossa restaurant, tipped off by a certain Concettina, to meet with a certain Masaniello, who played the accordion in a restaurant in Mergellina, come on, you could have reached your objective without resorting to such clichés, but I have to hand it to you, you did succeed, Masaniello did have some information, because you know, one Naples password is *vox populi*, and you wandered distracted and abandoned, and, with Masaniello's information, you managed to get to Vesuviano, to the Red Moon Center; you poor guy, your information was vague, but you did manage to reach your Luna Rossa.

He ground the cigarette butt into the sand and asked: should I go on? Go on, I said, I'm curious. Okay, he went on, long ago, after you found two or three idiot secretaries, you finally arrived at an old attendant who'd been their secretary years before, he was a scrawny little guy with glasses, god knows why he was still kept there, seeing how the Center had become so powerful it was even funded now by the State, maybe because they considered him some sort of military surplus, but he remembered Isabel, and he recognized her in that photo you showed him, he told you about her, about when she'd stopped in the Red Moon, but he didn't tell you anything about her life, maybe because he didn't know anything, but he did give you this address, this little Riviera train station, and he told you to go to Via Oberdan, to the Social Print Shop, because that was the last place Isabel was sent. He paused and looked at me. Why did you say this last part of my journey was long ago? I asked. He smiled and looked up at the sky. The distant past, he said, the near past, the present, the future, sorry, I don't really know tenses or time, it's all the same to me. I looked at him. He was rubbing his feet through the sand. But who are you? I asked. I'm the Mad Fiddler, he said, I'm the one directing your concentric circles, or your stations, if you prefer; and I too have been sent. Then, with his bow, he drew a small circle in the sand. We've reached the center, he whispered, give me Isabel's photo. I gave him the photo, and he laid it at the center of the circle. Then he stood up, raised his violin to his shoulder, and quietly began to play Beethoven's *Farewell Sonata*.

And right at that moment, I saw Isabel. She was walking up the slight hill, by the hedge; she was dressed in a blue silk gown, just as I saw her once at the City Hall, and she wore a small hat with a white veil. She held out her hand and I squeezed it; she raised her veil and I kissed her cheek. Hello, she said, as you can see, I still exist. I asked her to sit with me on the park bench. She held my hands in hers and said: come with me, I want to lead tonight. She slipped her arm in mine, like she used to. We walked down to the lane called Lavoratori del Mare. The fragrance of the pittosporum was intoxicating. Further down, you could see the lights of the gulf. Isabel, I said, where are you taking me? She brought her lips to my ear and whispered: wait, don't be so impatient. We continued down the hill.

The marina was deserted, the boats rocking gently on the water. On the far side of the marina, off the pier, a boat taxi was docked, its lights ablaze. Isabel led me onto the pier.

I climbed on board first, then held out my hand to help her up. The boat taxi was completely empty. Isabel invited me to sit on the deck, in one of the blue-and-white folding chairs. We'll be comfortable here, Isabel said, we can look at the night sky. She tied a white scarf around her neck, waved slightly toward a star, and the boat, as if under a spell, without a sound, pulled away from the pier and glided off, toward the distant lights of the gulf. And just then, I thought I recognized that gulf and those lights, and growing nervous, I said: Isabel, where are we? We're in our then, she answered. I took hold of her hands and said: please, tell me what you mean. This boat taxi has passed through the fifth wall, Isabel answered, we're in our then – see? – those are the lights of Portinho da Arrábida, we left from Setúbal, we're in the boat taxi that took us from Setúbal to Portinho da Arrábida, this is the night we said goodbye, on the boat taxi that night, don't you remember? We're in our then. But this can't be now and then at the same time, I said, Isabel, that's not possible, we're in our now right now. Now and then have been erased, Isabel answered, you're saying goodbye to me like you did back then, but we're in our present, it's the present for us both, and you're saying goodbye. All right,

I said, if I have to tell you goodbye in our then, I want to know what your life's been like.

The lights of Arrábida were drawing closer. The boat taxi sounded its whistle, youu-youu, it called. Otherwise that warm night was quiet. Isabel smiled at me and squeezed my hand. Her white scarf fluttered in the night breeze. What's the point of telling you about my life? she said, you know everything already, you've formed your circles with great skill, you know everything about me, my life was exactly like that, I ran away toward nothing, and I made it through, now you've found me in your last circle, but you need to know: your center is my nothing, the place I find myself now, I wanted to disappear into nothing, and I succeeded, and now you've found me in this nothing, with your astral drawing, but there's something you need to know, you didn't find me, I found you – you think your search for me is over, but you were only searching for yourself. What do you mean, Isabel? I asked. She squeezed my hand hard. I mean that you wanted to free yourself from your remorse, it wasn't so much that you were searching for me as for yourself, to pardon yourself, a pardon and an answer, and I'm giving you that answer tonight, the night we said goodbye on a boat taxi going from Setúbal to Arrábida, you're released from all your guilt, you're not guilty of anything, Tadeus, there's no little bastard child of yours in the world, you can go in peace, your mandala's complete. All right, I said, but Isabel, where are you, in this now of yours? If you walk up the narrow road leading from the Riviera station where you arrived, she said, halfway up the hill, you'll find a very small cemetery, and down the central path, in among the plainest graves, there's one that no one visits, with a few wrought-iron flowers and a simple headstone that has no dates, no photograph, just an epitaph that reads: here lies Isabel known as Magda, come from afar and longing for peace. That's where you lie? I asked. No, she said, that's a cenotaph, just the memory of what was, two simple names, the essence of a life, I'm in nothing, and like I said before: you mustn't feel any regrets, rest in peace on your constellation, while I continue along my path in my nothing.

The boat taxi docked on the Arrábida pier. Clouds hung heavy over the gulf; I felt the first drops of rain. Isabel pulled a very light raincoat from her bag and put it on. This is just like the night we said goodbye, do you remember? It was raining. Isabel, wait, I said, you can't say goodbye another time. Isabel stood, and she leaned over and kissed me. Goodbye, Tadeus, she said, this is the last time, we most certainly won't see each other again, goodbye. And she walked away, like I saw her walk away that night, down the short pier, down to a restaurant with a pale neon moon, and at a distance, she pulled her scarf from her neck and waved it goodbye, one last time. I said goodbye as well, timidly, waving, though my hand was hidden in my lap.

I opened my eyes. The violinist was standing in front of me in that garden by the station; the moon had set. Violin on his shoulder, he stared at the circle in the sand by his bare foot. And now it's time to go back, he said, your search is through. He squatted and blew on the sand. The circle was erased. Why'd you do that? I asked. Because your search is through, he said, and it takes a puff of wind to lead everything back to the wisdom of nothing. I picked up the photograph of Isabel and put it in my pocket. I'll take this along, I said. Go right ahead, he told me, it's your right, sometimes a picture is all that remains of everything. He raised his violin to his shoulder and began playing softly, very sweetly, *Les Adieux, l'Absence, le Retour*. I looked up at the sky and saw a familiar star. I started on my way. And at that moment, I saw Isabel. She was waving a white scarf and saying goodbye.

Translator's Acknowledgments

I wish to thank Jill Schoolman, publisher of Archipelago Books, for everything she does for international literature and for translators. I've consulted with numerous translators – from Italian, Portuguese, German, and Chinese – about details of this novel; many thanks to everyone. I also wish to express my deep gratitude to my friend and colleague Louise Rozier, for her insights into the original novel and for her meticulous feedback about my translation. Finally, I want to thank Scott Kallstrom, whose support and enthusiasm for my work mean all the world to me.